"A raw book of great power."
—*Voice Literary Supplement*

"In her first novel, Grant emerges as a stylish writer. More significantly, though, she proves a valuable observer of the present age, skillfully transforming the fodder for countless TV movies into an innovative and often satirical exploration of Americans' faith in the recovery process. . . . Her novel is a timely debut of fresh insight and considerable heart."
—*Washington City Paper*

"[An] accomplished first novel."
—*The New Yorker*

The Passion of Alice

Stephanie Grant

BANTAM BOOKS
NEW YORK • TORONTO • LONDON • SYDNEY • AUCKLAND

THE PASSION OF ALICE

A Bantam Book

PUBLISHING HISTORY

*Previously published in hardcover by
Houghton Mifflin Company in 1995*

Bantam trade paperback edition / October 1996

ISBN 0-553-37861-9

Published simultaneously in the United States and Canada

*Bantam Books are published by Bantam Books, a division of Bantam Doubleday
Dell Publishing Group, Inc. Its trademark, consisting of the words "Bantam
Books" and the portrayal of a rooster, is Registered in U.S. Patent and Trademark
Office and in other countries. Marca Registrada. Bantam Books, 1540 Broadway,
New York, New York 10036.*

PRINTED IN THE UNITED STATES OF AMERICA

FFG   10 9 8 7 6 5 4 3 2 1

For my mother,
Edna Katherine MacNeill Grant
and for my sister,
Jaime Marie Grant,
who, between them,
have given me the world.

Life is short, but desire, desire is long.
JANE HIRSHFIELD, *Heat*

Inside every fat woman is a fatter one.
BARBARA GOLDBERG, *Superego Serenade*

The
Passion
of
Alice

Prologue

We wait for epiphanies. Grouped in circles, seated on folding metal chairs, or cross-legged on foam mats on the floor, we wait for moments of insight and self-clarification. They come regularly. Not unlike how salvation in evangelical churches must come. First a strained silence. Then a flutter, a flap of ugly words rushing in the room like wind, a halting confession. Then contagion.

We wait to find out the thing that is wrong with each of us. What happened. When and how the damage was done. Who has been the instrument, who has turned some simple lack or some not-so-simple excess into self-hate. Lack and excess, these are the tickets: who would have thought moderation would prove so essential? Enough love, but not too much. Enough discipline, but not too much. Enough morality, but not too much.

The therapists are like tuning forks for epiphanies. In individual, they hammer *and then, and then*, and *how did that make you feel*? But in group therapy, they demonstrate their true genius, quietly inciting multiple confessions from a single wormy word. Shame. Fault. Responsibility. Father. Brother. Mother. The truth is, everyone blames somebody. Everyone pretends that being here is not, somehow, her doing.

I have tried to explain my own point of view to the counselors, but they won't listen. They see us as persons without free will. Incapable of choice. They have neat square boxes for everything in their world, and I must fit in the box that says self-starving equals self-hate.

They could not be more wrong.

My anorexia is a form of self-knowledge. People think that anorexics imagine ourselves fat and diet away invisible flab. But people are afraid of the truth: we prefer ourselves this way, boiled-down bone, essence. My favorite cooking metaphor (unfortunate perhaps) applies: not reduce, *clarify*. I know exactly what I look like, without hyperbole. Every inch of skin, each muscle, each bone. I see where and how they connect. I can name the tendons and the joints. I finger the cartilage. When I eat, I follow the food as it digests, watching the lump of carrot or rice cake diminish, until, finally, elimination.

This is what sets us apart—apart from the rest of the world and apart from the other women here. Anorexics differentiate between desire and need. Between want and must. Just to know where I begin and end seems, in this day and age, a remarkable spiritual achievement. Why relinquish that? Why aspire to less? Why assimilate?

They have a narrow Christian idea of the spiritual at Seaview. My anorexia is religious in the Eastern sense that to know oneself completely and truly is to know God. In the early days of Christianity, there was an offshoot of Catholicism that focused on knowledge over faith. They called themselves Gnostics. They were champions of individual interpretations of Christ's story; they believed in the Resurrection as metaphor.

At Seaview, the counselors take Resurrection quite literally. In fact, they take everything literally, which is what makes them so humorless. They have relinquished their imaginations in favor of a belief in their power to resurrect us, to bring back our old selves, from *before*. This is called Recovery.

But I am committed to the Gnostic tenet that says

my own experience, my own insights, are as significant as the beliefs of the Orthodox, who simply have the good fortune of being in power. And like the Gnostics before me, I continue to believe in my own capacity for the divine.

PART

I

One

The bathroom door was locked. I asked Nurse to open it after my interview with Dr. Paul. She handed me my travel bag and took a wad of keys from the deep front pocket of her nurse's overalls, where they had been making holes in the polyester. She wheeled me over the threshold and stopped the chair. Her broad white back held the door ajar. I hesitated. I had hoped she would wheel me all the way to the handicapped stall, the fourth in a row after three narrower stalls. It stood big and roomy as a house, the boltless door slapped open. Even from where we waited, I could see the fat chrome rails inside.

"We haven't got all day," Nurse said.

I put the cloth bag on the floor (Syd had packed some everyday clothes, not just nighties) and pushed the blankets from my lap. I disentangled my feet. The hospital johnny did not reach my knees. I glanced over my shoulder. Nurse was staring out the bathroom door, purposefully ignoring my bare thighs and the booties—part sock, part slipper—that had fallen around my ankles. I pulled them up and lifted myself out of the chair. The white tile cold seeped through the wool.

I touched the sinks opposite the stalls, my fingertips grazing the chill porcelain, my gray eyes following the image in the mirrors. The nurses at Medical had said my eyes were my best feature; I'd always thought it was my hair, pitch-black and wavy, even in the worst of circumstances. At the end of the row, the handicapped stall had its own matching dwarfed sink with a slanted mirror that exposed my ankles and calves. I couldn't remember the last time I'd shaved.

"I bet the big ones go in there," I said, pointing to the too-spacious stall. Nurse drummed her fingers against the heavy wood door.

I sat on my hands on the bowl in the third stall, too weak to hover, and strained to pee without splash, in a tight, straight stream. Nurse pretended not to hear.

"Dr. Paul is a creep," I said after flushing.

Nurse shrugged. "Worse than some, better than others."

When I climbed back into the wheelchair, the metal footrest scraped a veil of skin from my calf. I leaned over and rubbed away the sting. Tomorrow I would have a violet bruise. "He has fat hands," I said.

Nurse tucked the blanket around my legs and gave me back the bag. Her hands were long-fingered, with big red knuckles. She was my favorite nurse at Medical, unobtrusive and honest. During my three weeks there, she had never lied about what would hurt or who would be in charge. I called her Nurse because she seemed the incarnation of her job. When the time came for the transfer to Psychiatric, I requested that she be the one to wheel me.

Nurse backed the chair expertly out of the bathroom and down the hall to the elevator. I could see the door to Dr. Paul's office, where I had had my exam. ADMITTING it said in big block letters, DR. P. SAMPSON, M.D. Syd was still in there, getting—I didn't know what—last-minute, mother-of-the-sick instructions.

He had not said much to me during the physical. Syd had waited in his outer office while his cherub's hands roamed my body in the examining room, checking heart, lungs, blood pressure. He tapped my chest and back as if looking for hidden beams in an old house.

"Everything's where it should be," he said, raising his eyebrows.

I didn't laugh.

After, in the outer office, he made me climb on the scale in front of Syd. It was an old-fashioned doctor's scale, shaped like a giant letter T, with a metal arm for measuring height and a thick metal platform to stand on. I held my johnny closed in back and stepped up. My toes curled inside the booties.

The first surprise was that I'd shrunk a quarter of an inch: five foot ten and three-quarters. No one but me was alarmed. Dr. Paul fiddled with the weights, starting first with the hundred-pound block, then putting it back and moving the smaller pieces. "Ninety-four and a quarter," he said, without waiting for the lever to come to a balance.

Syd looked like she'd taken a wrong turn. "What is that, Dr. Sampson, metric?"

His eyebrows raised again. That was when he insisted we call him Paul, both of us, of course, but it was meant for Syd. He went over to his wide oak desk and plucked a lime green folder from a multicolored pile. He smiled at her.

"Alice was admitted at ninety-two, lost three and a half from the initial trauma, then after a week of intravenous TPN and another week of liquid food, she's back up to, what did I say?" He looked at me, then over to Syd. "Ninety-four and a quarter. *Pounds*, Mrs. Forrester."

It was the first I'd heard about breaking ninety.

Syd leaned forward in her chair. Her eyes climbed past my ankles, knees, crepe-skinned thighs, and white johnny. She stopped at my bony face. Her pupils shrank. It was the first time in three years that she saw what I looked like. What I weighed. It wasn't that she hadn't known I was anorexic. She just hadn't seen.

Dr. Paul came out from behind his desk. He patted her slim hand with his fat one. He said, "Sometimes, these things are hardest on the family members."

·   ·   ·

When the elevator pinged open, Nurse pulled me to one side, letting the riders spill out, then backed me into the beige box—so far the only walls in the hospital not ultra-white. Before the elevator doors closed, I saw Syd and Dr. Paul emerge from his office. He was maybe a head shorter than she, longish hair starting in wisps around his ears, the bald dome shiny, his face professional and penitent, as if *he* had something to be sorry for. Syd was looking smart and alert in a pin-striped suit with slacks. If you didn't know her well, you couldn't tell she had just had shattering news; but then, you couldn't tell a lot of things about my mother from looking at her. In the last sliver of light before the doors shut, I could make out Dr. Paul's pink hand cupped around her elbow.

Two

The fortunate thing was that my father's law firm had handled Seaview's tax problems for the last five years. The more fortunate thing, however, was that one of my father's associates, and not my father, had done the work, so no one in administration recognized the name when I was admitted. It meant we had the advantage, my family and I, of knowing their history without their knowing ours.

Dad said Seaview's three identical brick buildings—the Medical Hospital, the Research Building, and the Psychiatric Hospital—were built in 1957, a dozen years after the armistice. Psychiatry was enjoying an unexpected boom then; Betty Friedan's housewives and recalcitrant veterans sought help in great numbers. The Seaview Complex was an experiment; the close proximity of the three buildings allowed researchers regular access to their patients so they could better study the connections between mental and physical illness. But by the late sixties, it was clear the experiment had failed. The researchers didn't like the patients, or there weren't enough of them with the same illness for a proper study; and the patients detested the researchers, who, they complained, kept trying to get them to fill out questionnaires.

Dad gave me all the details on the day it was decided about the transfer to Psychiatric. I wasn't exactly committed; but the doctors made it clear that I would be if I didn't volunteer. Dad had brought his work file on Seaview to my room in cardiac care and read me excerpts. My father and I liked having lots of information; it made us feel better. He and Syd and I pretended it was our decision. It was the first time since the divorce that I could remember them not fighting.

In 1973, Seaview Psychiatric became an alcohol and drug rehabilitation center, dropping substance-free lunatics for more lucrative addicts. The Research Building began to focus on developing better detox drugs and the Medical Hospital pretty much stayed the same, catering to the general health needs of Marshfield's middle class. The eating disorder unit was not established until 1980. It was the only treatment facility of its kind on the south shore of Boston, not quite halfway between the city and Cape Cod. When I got there, in 1984, business was good.

Seaview's triple-fold promotional brochure featured a turquoise seahorse on the front flap and two pictures of local beaches on the inside. But there was no view of the sea. Not from inside any of the buildings. The brochure said Seaview Psychiatric was "elegant" with "state-of-the-art" facilities. Perhaps in 1957. Not that it was threadbare now. But function had clearly overtaken form, with big-ticket items like twin bed sets bought in bulk.

I was lucky, everyone said after the heart attack, the way people do when something terribly unlucky, something catastrophic, has happened. I was lucky to have been brought to Seaview, instead of the Goddard or Carney hospitals, both of which were closer to the South Shore Plaza in Braintree, where I collapsed. Syd and I had been working the Presidents' Day sales that Monday, and when the paramedics gave Syd a choice, she chose Goddard because my brother and I had been born there. Which was when, according to family friends, my extreme good luck came in: there had been an accident, a big one, a dozen cars on Route 24, a few minutes from Goddard. We didn't get the call until we were halfway, the dispatcher's voice squawking high and excited over the radio. I remembered because I was trying to concentrate on any sound that was not Syd's crying. Goddard's emergency room was full. They couldn't admit us. It would have taken too long to drive back to Carney. We ended up at Seaview, another ten minutes farther east on Route 123. There, it turned out, the cardiologists in Medical—because of the nearness of Psychiatric—were experienced at working with slender young girls whose hearts had given out.

Three

We were allowed to walk to the cafeteria ourselves, using the staircase in the middle of the floor next to the nurses' station. On my first full day, Janine, my roommate, escorted me. It was large, like a school or a corporate cafeteria, with linoleum floors and flat squares of fluorescent light suspended overhead. But instead of the standard Formica tables and folding chairs, there was real furniture.

We chose from three breakfast entrees at a big serving window. It reminded me of high school. Ladies in pink smocks and hairnets stood behind the open window and pushed trays toward us. We walked by single file and picked either poached eggs on wheat toast, cinnamon-apple oatmeal, or corn flakes with banana. Janine explained that at lunch and dinner we got special trays with our names on them, but at breakfast they tried to force us to be responsible for what we ate by giving us a choice. I asked for a fresh bowl of cereal, one without the milk already poured. A lunchroom lady went in the back and brought me out a dry bowl and a little glass of milk.

"There you go, doll," she said.

"Skim?"

She smiled and crossed her arms. "That's all we got here, honey, is skim."

Janine waved from one of the tables. "I saved you a seat." She pointed to a stout red armchair with cushions. "Grab that one." Her mouth already full of oatmeal.

I rested my tray on the table and used both hands to pull out the chair. No two were alike; they came from the different rooms of a house: kitchen, living, den. Janine sat in a maple captain's chair.

"The armchairs are the most popular," she said.

I knew I was supposed to be grateful. Probably this was how Janine made friends, by cultivating indebtedness. True, she'd been assigned to shepherd me, but I could tell she liked it. I looked around the room. A dozen or so mis-shapen girls made their way toward homely kitchen tables. I hoped nobody sat with us. My roommate's jabbering was enough.

I mashed the corn flakes along the bottom of my bowl while Janine recounted everything she'd learned in her five weeks at Seaview; she hoped to leave in less than ten days if all went well. She told me it was perfectly okay to be afraid. "Everyone's scared at first," she said.

"But I'm not afraid," I said. "Not the way the others are." In my first twenty-four hours, I hadn't cried once be-cause I didn't feel sorry for myself. Or for them. We'd chosen what we'd chosen, after all. I said, "I'm only afraid of getting fat."

Janine looked down at her oatmeal, her smug chaper-on's smile collapsing.

Her clothes fit tight. She'd probably gained weight since coming here.

I wondered whose plan was it anyway, to lump us all together? The obese alongside the thinning. The morn-ing's first activity had been a public meditation. There we were, every girl who'd ever been tortured at recess. We rolled around on mats in a rectangular room at the end of the hall. Mary Beth, the exercise physiologist, led us through some basic yoga moves. She made us face east for the Saluta-tion to the Sun. We had to imagine the sun, though. The windows were hidden by dove gray drapes. On my left and two mats behind, the fattest girl I'd ever seen wheezed. I wanted a better look, but couldn't exactly crane my neck;

east was east, and the giantess sat west. Still, I couldn't shake the thought: what could we offer each other outside of cruelty?

The only interesting piece of news from Janine was that both the showers and the bathrooms were locked.

"Why the showers?"

Her smile returned. Janine had an optimistic look: the tightest possible ponytail, high cheekbones, and expensive makeup. She could throw a baton. "The water covers the sound," she said.

"So that explains the nurse standing vigil?"

"Yep."

I pictured Janine naked and ponytailed, crouching low to the drain. "So you're—"

"Bulimic and anorexic," she said.

"Both?"

"Both."

"I thought they were a contradiction in terms."

"It's new, but very common," she said. "You're what then, purely anorexic?"

"Uh-huh."

"You're the rarity these days. More of us are both."

"No kidding." I had thought you either ate too much or didn't eat. I had thought that was the basic distinction.

"I was into these New Age health diets," she said. "They were strictly deprivation diets in disguise. No sugar, no white flour, no dairy, no red meat, no caffeine. No toxins whatsoever."

I wanted to ask about the throwing up, but Janine did not wait for questions.

"I ate very healthy. Vegetable juices and wheat grass, steamed vegetables and brown rice. Seaweed. Once in a while a free-range chicken. You know, the ones without the hormones. And lots of miso soup."

I realized everyone would be eager to tell the thing she did with food. Like the way girls talked about masturbation in college. I felt old-fashioned explaining I was a simple calorie counter. Not that I hadn't eaten Janine's way for a while. I'd eaten every way, for a while. But over the years, I returned to straight calorie counting. Five hundred a day to maintain, four hundred to lose. I liked the control, the absolute ability to quantify my intake. No surprises. No need to purge. I tried to keep it simple, which was funny because that was one of Seaview's insipid slogans. If I managed what came in, I could manage what went out. No drama, no mess.

Janine pointed at my bowl of cereal. "You don't have to do that."

"Do what?"

"Hide your food."

The corn flakes were covered by milk.

"They don't force us to eat. They don't even particularly supervise our eating. See that counselor." She indicated a squat woman in a flowered dress. "That's Gert. She's on duty."

Gert was walking from table to table, chatting, her chin forward, her hands clasped behind her back. She looked at faces, not plates.

"She notices what you eat, but they won't do anything about it for a while. They have this theory that after two weeks, you'll come around."

"What happens if you don't?"

Janine shrugged, her face flaming a little at the outer edges.

I said, "Do they force-feed you?"

"Not exactly."

"What then?"

She searched the room. Her eyes settled on someone. "See that young girl at the table nearest the serving window."

I turned around. There was a kid sitting in a kitchen chair. Her feet hung just above the black-and-white linoleum; if she flexed her toes, they would reach. Someone's little sister, I had thought.

"Amy's been here three months. They won't let her leave until she makes a certain weight."

"How old is she?"

"Thirteen."

"No way."

"Suit yourself."

"She looks ten, eleven tops."

"I know. There's talk she may have permanently stunted her growth."

"She's built like a ruler."

"You don't have to tell me."

There was something in her voice. I turned around. Janine was not built like a ruler, more like a pear. Perhaps she had come in like a ruler. She said, "Amy's even got her own room."

"Her own room? I thought everyone shared."

Janine shook her head. "She started out with a roommate, but they moved her."

"Why's that?"

"Who knows." Janine looked away.

I wondered if she could see it. My desire taking form. I hated for people to know what I wanted. Our room was torpedo-shaped, with barely enough space between the twin beds to pass. Last night I had listened to her not snore; whenever she was on the brink, whenever her breath had gotten thick, she'd switched sides.

"She must be pretty crazy, that Amy," I said, "to get her own room."

Janine looked at me and sighed. "I just don't think Amy wants to get better."

I nodded soberly.

"And that's the only thing they ask." Her voice thinned with emotion. "That we want to get better."

"Sounds reasonable," I said, thinking about a private room, dreaming about what I would ask and how. But I knew even then: it was not a thing to *ask*.

Four

After breakfast there was a lecture on nutrition and general health care. Imagine teaching people who jam their fingers down their throats—or eat until they pass out, or don't eat until they pass out—about nutrition. "Vitamins and the Immune System." As if all we lacked was knowledge.

Two of the women were actually nutritionists themselves, Janine and this one old lady. I watched them dream up intricate questions about food combining and amino acids, their hands shooting into the air when they thought they had a stumper. The older woman was big into laxatives and colonics. Purification, she called it. She was still bloated and slightly orange from the laxatives. She'd been taking about twenty a day. Her name was Victoria, but they called her Queen Victoria because she was so old, sixty at least. She carried pictures of her grandchildren with her in a wallet-size photo album that said "Crazy Old Grandma with Pictures in Her Purse" on the cover. It was red vinyl with gold lettering and closed with a snap.

From nutrition we went to art therapy. Although we didn't actually go anywhere. A tone marked the end of the period. Not a bell. It had a neutral sound, like the beep of those new phone systems. At the tone, we left the group room and stood outside for several minutes while they switched instructors and moved furniture. There was no time to do anything except look at Queen Victoria's pictures. Almost all the kids were at that age of missing teeth.

Back inside, the art therapist paired us up according to disorder. We made a twisted line, bingers with bingers, starvers with starvers, vomiters with vomiters. There was one girl left over, the big wheezer I'd listened to in meditation. The art therapist—her name was Cass—volunteered to be her partner. We got huge scrolls of grainy paper, two per couple. Cass said we would be making life-size drawings of our bodies. They could be realistic or fantastic, whatever we wanted. The only thing she insisted be true to life was the original outline. We took positions on the floor, leaving space enough for Cass to pass between us. We overflowed into the hall. Half of us lay down on the sheets while the other half traced our outlines. The corners of the paper curled at our feet and our heads until we weighted them down with each other's shoes.

I had hoped Amy would be my partner—I wanted to ask what she'd done to get a single room—but she hadn't come to art therapy. Cass said Amy had already completed two body drawings during the three months of her stay. I wondered where she'd gone instead. Cass introduced me to a pasty anorexic named Gwen.

"Guinevere?" I asked.

She shook her head no, but she looked the part. The type that wouldn't drink tap water, not even boiled for tea. And bath oil pearls in every bath. Like the ones I'd made my little brother Alex eat when he was three. Syd kept them arranged in wooden bowls, like fruit, along the rim of her tub.

"Gwendolyn?"

She nodded, and her white-blond hair began to pull away from its French braid. She held herself gingerly, as if she were connected by threads.

Gwen crouched by my ear and moved around me on the floor, breathing audibly as she traced the outline. I made a jumping jack with my body: hands together above my head, feet apart. I closed my eyes. The paper was coarse against the backs of my hands. My shoulder blades and tailbone poked through paper to the flat gray carpet underneath. Gwen moved around my feet. She wasn't a talker. I opened one eye. The line she drew was barely legible, the paper just registering the pressure of her pencil. I followed her progress up the other shin, around my knee. She was careful not to touch me, probably hating the feel of flesh as much as I. Maybe that was why they lumped us together according to disorder.

She ended at my hands, taking time with the fingers. When she stood, she murmured something.

"Pardon me?" I got up to look.

Lovely wrists. She mouthed the words.

We stared at the drawing. My slinky wrists looked bound above my head.

"Aristocratic," she said softly, wetting her lips with a pointed tongue.

I was almost certainly the thinnest woman here.

Gwen's outline took me half the time to draw, partly because I was taller and could walk more quickly around, but also because she kept her hands at her sides and her legs tight together. I had less area to cover.

When we finished, Cass gave a speech. She pushed her long, unstyled gray hair behind her ears, exposing droopy breasts. She was wearing an earth-colored artist's smock and espadrilles.

"Today, my dears, you are to begin work on filling in these body drawings. Use whatever you like—watercolors, pen and ink, charcoal, collage, sequins, feathers. Anything goes." Cass crossed to the wood cabinets that lined one wall. She unlocked them with a key she wore on a leather string around her neck. "I want you to investigate each box, contemplate the materials. But no filling in yet, just thinking."

We placed the boxes of sticky supplies between our outlines on the floor. Gwen divulged her preliminary plan: patent leather shoes. She rifled through the miscellaneous box for shiny material that would pass. Someone suggested duct tape. The wheezer, Louise, apparently a friend of Gwen's, reappeared. Cass had traced her outline in the hall. I'd never understood how fat people got their strange physiques, why the weight didn't distribute itself evenly, why it usually collected in one or more distorted body part. Louise was diamond-shaped, with a great big ring of fat at her hips, her layered flesh tapering toward her head and feet. She forced her way in front of me in order to be next to Gwen, her movement more side to side than straight ahead. The group walked in a snaking line, stepping shoeless around our flattened selves.

Not that I cared that Gwen and Louise were friends. It wasn't as if I'd planned on being Gwen's pal any more than I'd planned on being Louise's. In a room of a hundred people, they would have been the last two I'd have sought. Why pretend otherwise, just because of circumstance? What surprised me mostly was that Gwen didn't seem to mind Louise. Or was too mousy to object.

After we'd contemplated materials for half an hour, Cass gathered us together in a circle to talk about our plans. She said we could sit on the mats we had used at our morning meditation. Apparently most of our activities would take place here, in the group room. It was large, with folding chairs and mats and whatever supplies thought necessary stored in the wood cabinets. The wall facing the cabinets was all windows. Not the meager portholes we had in our rooms. Real windows that started at your knees and reached up to the ceiling. There should have been lots of light at all of our activities, but so far, there hadn't been. They kept the drapes closed. I asked the meditation lady why and she said for warmth and privacy. Which seemed absurd. As if anyone would have wanted to peek inside. More likely they had grown used to controlling our environment and did it now reflexively. Control, even by degrees, was pleasurable. They enjoyed keeping us in dim light.

Cass opened the drapes for our discussion. "Light

changes everything," she said, "not just how we see things, but how things are."

Watery March light streamed in, stinging our eyes, forcing us to squint or to make hoods with our hands. We looked pale, tubercular. Even the fattest ones.

Five

It took me less than four days to divine the different schools of thought at Seaview. Not that they were so hard to figure: the counselors hardly hid their ideologies. The predominant point of view was Twelve Step, which said simply that food, and what you did with it, could be addictive. Since a rose was a rose was a rose, the treatment was the same as for alcoholics and drug addicts, although slightly complicated by the fact that the substance (alas) could never be entirely forsaken. We attended at least one Twelve Step meeting a day, as well as step-writing workshops. The famous steps hung on large placards on the walls in every treatment room. The most oft-repeated slogans were embroidered, like kitchen samplers, on tiny plaques and pillows in our bedrooms. I couldn't help but notice when I got there, people talked funny. The constant repetition of certain phrases was positively Jim Jonesian.

The second theory borrowed more from Freud than Bill W. and Dr. Bob. It said eating disorders were only a symptom of a greater psychological disturbance. Cure the real problem, and the food obsession would go away. This theory was not as incompatible with Twelve Step doctrine as it first appeared. Gert, the head Twelve Stepper, said addiction was a physical, spiritual, and emotional disease that had to be attacked on all fronts simultaneously. Thus, shrinkage was not only encouraged, it was mandated. All of which accounted for the endless parade of individual and group and family group therapies we attended. About this much they all agreed: it would be a talking cure.

Finally there was the feminist point of view, at best marginal at Seaview. Dana, my shrink for individual, was its champion. The basic idea was that when women began taking up more public space in the early 1970s, during and after the women's movement—public space being the workplace, politics, the nightly news—they gradually were required to take up less private space. In other words, women had to be physically smaller at home, in the kitchen, and between the sheets. It was a nice, neat theory. Twiggy was popular about then. The big girls loved it because the treatment line was to stop dieting, stop trying to change your shape. We were all as we were meant to be, a variety of sizes, not a single and singular ideal. But most of us wouldn't touch it. I could almost see the collective thought forming: there go the feminists again, rationalizing unsightliness.

Not that I didn't consider myself a feminist. I did. But like most women my age, I could pick it up and put it down. And then, I was also Catholic. A convert in my adolescence, though no longer practicing by the time I got to Seaview. Which meant, being a feminist and a Catholic (it never really left me, practicing or not), I could hold two opposing ideas about something in my head at the same time.

Not surprisingly, our days at Seaview were very structured. After lunch we had food group, where we talked about—you can't make this up—what we'd just eaten. When all of our trays had been returned, they pushed aside the cafeteria tables and we pulled our chairs together in a loose circle. The lunchroom ladies closed the serving window, lowering the partition like a shade, and cleaned unobserved by us, though we could hear their noise from the hidden kitchen, nasal South Shore accents that lifted over the whoosh of the commercial dishwasher, the tinkle of flatware against glass, and the scruff of the big push brooms. They were comforting noises. The only comfort during food group.

We smelled the next day's soup while we talked about how it felt to taste, swallow, and digest food. Vegetable soup usually. No potatoes, but cabbage, onion, carrot, and celery so soft it was the easiest to mush against the side of the bowl. A hint of black pepper. Today we'd had chicken noodle, and I could still taste the chicken fat on my lips. I kept wiping my mouth with the napkin I'd saved. The bulimics were particularly distraught at this hour. They couldn't stand having anything inside their bodies. Physically feeling the food in their throats and esophagi was torture without the promise of release. They pointed to where the food got stuck, above the breastbone, at the triangular indent where the clavicles converge. They rubbed their fingers in the triangle, the way you rub a cat's throat to make it swallow a pill. They couldn't sit still.

Gert began. "Okay, who's first?"

"I was fine, absolutely fine. I felt hungry, then full. It was nothing but food."

"Good, Janine."

Everyone hated her, not just me. It was like she was running for class president. She never said a wrong thing.

"Anyone else?" said Gert.

Louise began to cry.

Gert let her go on for a while. They loved it when you cried. Then, "Can you tell us why you're crying? Why you're sad?"

Louise refused to lift her head. Her choppy brown hair hung in front of her face, sticking to the wetness. She had a bad fat person's hairdo: blunt cut, but at an angle so that it was shortest at the nape of her neck and longest by her face, leaving the ropes of fat at her neck exposed. It was meant to frame her blotchy face, give it shape somehow, but that was impossible. Louise's face was endless, a face within a face within a face.

"I know it's hard to give things up," said Gert.

All the counselors were recovering from their own eating disorders. Unlike real-world shrinks, they loved to tell their personal stories, which were supposed to be inspirational. And because they had gone through the same process, they were thought to be more empathetic.

"Familiar things, especially," said Gert. "I remember when I stopped drinking, it was like I was losing my best friend." Gert was known to be dually addicted—food and alcohol—which gave her a certain stature.

Louise suddenly began talking about her parents. Mom was a brilliant astronomer, Dad an advanced calculus teacher. Both college professors, but Mom the celebrity. Louise wailed about the trials of being the nongifted daughter of a onetime child prodigy who'd scored "borderline genius" on the Mensa test. She made disgusting snuffly noises until Gwen handed her a tissue.

Gert was pleased. Non sequiturs were prized at Seaview, especially ones that revealed some personal trauma. Ask a patient how she did in high school; if she answers that her brother tried to drown her in the bathtub when she was three, you know it's straight from the UC—the unconscious. Sometimes, before our meetings, we did what they called guided visualizations in order to call up the UC. Apparently, the unconscious was either a room at the end of a long corridor or a private grotto that only you knew about.

Louise's outburst proved to be the high point of food group. The compulsive eaters sulked through the hour. You could tell they thought they were being starved. The bulimics were the only ones who talked, but they kept their eyes on the door. The anorexics said nothing, humiliated at having been seen eating. Gwen wouldn't look at anyone except Louise. Amy occupied herself with the hem of her plaid skirt. I was quiet, in comparatively minimal distress. I wasn't eating all my food at meals. I hadn't yet. I gave whatever I could to Louise.

The thing we did was quick, clean. I mashed the soft

foods first—rice, peas, beans. The vegetables were always a notch past al dente. The chicken cutlet (or hamburger, or fish filet) I chopped into tiny bite-size pieces. Food looked smaller cut. I saved the big items for her—potato, roll, dessert. These I slipped down my stretch-waist pants and tucked into the side of my underwear.

The young nurse whose chair propped open the bathroom door was usually reading trash: *The Other Side of the Moon/Mountain/Magic/Midnight*. We talked about books while I waited in line. She was my age. She preferred historical romances. The line grew. Louise was two people behind.

Inside, I stacked a pyramid of carbohydrates on the toilet paper dispenser and waited until Louise's surprisingly tiny feet appeared under the door of my stall. I flushed and unlatched. Louise did not look up as she rushed past me.

Most people believed that anorexics only hate fat on their own bodies. Most people were wrong.

Six

———

Sunday was Palm Sunday, and I asked to go to Mass in the chapel located inside the Medical Building. My team was surprised by the request. They didn't realize I was serious until I refused breakfast because of Communion. This caused quite a stir. They hunted down the Catholic doctors and nurses to confirm the orthodoxy of my pre-Communion fast. In high school, when I went to church regularly, I fasted from the night before, even though the Second Vatican Council had declared a one-hour fast sufficient way back in 1963. But whichever standard the doctors applied, I was safe: Mass began at nine and breakfast was at eight. They allowed me to stay in my room—with the proviso that I eat as soon as I return—while Janine and everyone else went down to the cafeteria. I left the door ajar and sat on my bed with my Bible open to the Book of Psalms. The other anorexics were furious. The real irony, I thought, was that I never read from Psalms, which, as a chapter, was sappy and overdone; I mostly read from the New Testament, and Psalms was in the Old, after Chronicles and before Proverbs. None of them knew that, though, walking by, so they couldn't see the humor in the situation, delicate perhaps, but there just the same. Louise tried to block Gwen's view of me when they passed, but I could see Gwen's white head bobbing.

Gert called over to Medical to let them know I was coming. Nurse, from cardiac care, met me at the hospital entrance, a sliding electronic glass door, at five minutes to nine. I could see the chapel's wooden archway from where I stood. It was the first thing you came to in the Medical Hospital, straight across from the Visitors' Information Desk and the gift shop, and before the long bank of elevators. During my stay at Medical, I hadn't visited the chapel once. Nurse was wearing her usual white overalls.

I said, "You're not coming inside."

She raised her shoulders, hardly a shrug.

I was wearing a favorite dirndl skirt for church, a navy blue linen, with taupe nylons and flats. (Sister Geraldine, my tutor for confirmation, had been firm in her preference for flesh-colored hosiery.) The nylons hung around my ankles—I was too tall for petites, my toes tore through, but mediums gathered like jowls around my ankles and knees. I kept tugging up the hose. It was one of the ways you could tell us converts from born Catholics: we dressed up.

Inside, the chapel was small and bright, the opposite of what I hoped for in a church. There were green and white palms in a basket by the door and, prematurely, lilies. Palm Sunday was a personal favorite. It marked the beginning of Holy Week, the seven most sacred days in the Catholic calendar, including what was known as the Passion of Christ. Not that I was fastidious about holy days of obligation anymore, but Mass still brought pleasure, especially the fancy ones, with incense and extra bells. Because it was Palm Sunday, everyone would get a palm on the way out.

Nurse stood by the last pew and waited for me to find a seat. I made my way to the second of the six pews, where I went down on one knee, then sat. Syd would have hated this church. Her interest was purely aesthetic: how would a bride look coming down the aisle? There was barely an aisle to speak of. A half-dozen steps and you were already at the phony altar, which had only one podium and no microphone.

There were five of us, not counting Nurse. Four women and a man. We each had a pew to ourselves. I wished I had worn a heavier skirt: the pew bit through the linen into the backs of my thighs, and I had to rearrange my weight, first on one buttock, then on the other, then evenly over the two. I could feel the bones in my back and legs; my coccyx was sore. The pews were tawny-colored oak, rock hard from infrequent use. At Most Precious Blood, the church where I was baptized and confirmed, the pews were the darkest mahogany, worn and yielding.

The priest arrived. There wasn't a side altar or a vestry; he walked down the same aisle that we had, stopping at the first pew to remove his black trench coat, folding it in half, then lengthwise. He was old, his hair an inch of stiff white; his movements were deliberate, economical. He was already wearing the alb, a cream tunic that dipped to his knees, but he pulled a purple stole from the pocket of the trench and draped it over his shoulders. He sighed as he took the single, high step up to the altar. Because he was small and hunched, he did not stand behind the podium where no one would have seen him. Instead he stood at the edge of the altar, his black shoes shining over the lip of the step, his arms raised. "Let us pray," he said. "In the name of the Father, Son, and Holy Ghost." He wasn't wearing any robes.

It was hard to take him or the Mass seriously in such a flimsy church. The walls were plaster, not stone, and the same brilliant white as the rest of the hospital. Fake stained-glass windows threw cartoon colors across the dull carpet. There were no statues. "Lord have mercy," he said.

Syd knew a thing or two about churches; she'd studied the way they were built. She chose our family church, First Presbyterian, from a book called *Outstanding New England Architecture.* It did not matter to her that it was forty-five minutes away. She taught me about stained glass. She said that no one made the real thing anymore, just painted glass. In every church we ever visited, Syd's first words to me were about the windows. She explained how to tell the difference: real stained glass was drab on the outside; it rewarded only those who came in.

On either side of the old priest sat two pots of lilies

and directly behind him hung a medium-size cross. I could smell the lilies. This time of year, most churches bought lilies that wouldn't bloom until Easter, but these were completely open and had already begun to die. The dark orange stamens stood stiff with pollen, the white petals had curled back toward the stalk, yellowing.

The priest cleared his throat and read from the Gospel According to Mark, skipping the Old Testament selections, then going straight into his sermon. He left out more than a quarter of the Mass. Apparently priests took liberties in hospital chapels, with no one there, official, to tell.

"The Easter season, spring, is a season of renewal." He looked at each of us, his eyes ash-dry. "Easter means that death is the antecedent to birth, instead of the other way around."

I couldn't tell if he believed what he was saying or not; some priests were obvious fakes. He looked more sad than anything. His face had aged into a permanent scowl, the corners of his lips turned down. I figured he had maybe been forced into semiretirement, relieved of his regular parish and demoted to saying Mass in the local hospitals and visiting the sick. Probably priests drew straws to determine who had to visit the sick and dying and were happy when some old guy got assigned the work. He probably spent most of his days administering last rites: blessing waxy faces either petrified with fear or already absent. Perhaps he carried a special bag, like a doctor's bag, filled with the holy items necessary for Catholic death—thick oil and incense and handmade cloths. He was so old himself, I wondered if he found the ritual comforting; I wondered what it was like for him to say the words over and over again, constantly accepting and preparing for loss; I wondered if he grieved.

I felt sorry for him, standing there bent over, working hard to come up with a good, convincing story, so I listened carefully, which was not my practice. Usually I read during the sermons. The ritual of the Mass itself, the story of the Crucifixion, these were what held my attention from the very start, not sermons. Too many priests explained their metaphors: Light bursting forth into darkness! Water cleansing the soul! The explanations ruined it. Right in my mouth, the blood would turn back into wine.

But this old guy was better than most. The gist of his sermon was that spring could be the most depressing time of year if you weren't experiencing renewal along with everyone and everything else. He said renewal was the real promise of the Resurrection.

Communion went fast. The five of us formed a puny line, one behind the other, mouths half open. We were not the type, not any of us, to receive the newfangled way, directly into our palms, the priest dropping the Host for us to retrieve ourselves; our fingers would never be clean enough for that. Back in our pews, we all tried to stretch the time, our faces plunged into cupped hands, our lips forming the longest prayers we knew. I wondered for whom the other four had come; for which elderly parent, for which unexpectedly sick sibling or spouse. The one man was smiling, fidgeting: his wife had just had their first son; he hadn't been in a church in years. I bet I was the only one there for myself, not making bargains. The Host stuck to the roof of my mouth. I left it there, undisturbed by my tongue. I would probably be back on the eating disorders unit when it finally melted.

The first time I took Communion at Most Precious Blood, the Host stuck to the roof of my mouth and I made great efforts to dislodge it. If what my new friend Ronald had explained to me was true, about transubstantiation and about the body and blood of Christ, it seemed untoward that Christ be jammed there. I ended by using my finger to scrape away the flattened wafer.

My decision to take Catholic Communion was impromptu. Ronald had been urging me to go to Mass, had said there was something about me—he couldn't say what exactly—that would be met in Catholic Church. (It was because he talked about things like *being met* that Ronald and I were becoming friends.) The long Communion lines at Most

Precious Blood were not what I was used to. At Syd's church, First Presbyterian, we passed around sturdy ceramic plates with cubes of soft white bread on them, and then a second round of plates that held Dixie cups filled with Welch's grape juice. The person next to you smiled when he handed you the plate. At Most Precious Blood, no one smiled during Communion. The church was intensely quiet, despite the movement of people into lines, the kneeling and standing, the coughs, baby cries, the hundreds of hands touching foreheads, then chests, then shoulders; it was as if they were willing the silence, holding it in their minds. The Communion line wound itself practically out of the church. The people walked slowly on the way to receive, then quickly back to their seats, afraid of losing what they'd just been given. I didn't know why I felt compelled to join them. When I finally got up front, I opened my mouth as wide as possible and the priest hesitated. I was apprehensive about him touching my tongue with his thumb, so I extended my tongue as far as it would go. He recovered from his start and delivered the Host, quick and practiced.

After Mass, Ronald confronted me in the church parking lot.

"It doesn't count, Alice," he said.

"What doesn't?"

"Communion. You shouldn't have gone. You have to be baptized."

"I am."

"Catholic. You have to be baptized Catholic."

"In our church, anyone who's Christian can take Communion."

"That's what the priest meant about being Catholic not being easy. There are rules."

"Sounds limiting to me. I would think they'd want anyone who was sincere."

Ronald looked at me before answering, his dark eyes brilliant against his dark face. "Well, they don't."

And that was the ultimate attraction of Catholicism—the exclusiveness. How difficult it was to really, really be a practicing Catholic. At the core of this difficulty lay transubstantiation. Catholics believed that the Communion bread became actual flesh for us to eat. Right there. Christ's real body; Christ's real blood. No metaphor. That's why the altar boy rang the bells; that's why the people in line for Communion looked so remorseful; that's why the priest couldn't get married (having a wife would ruin it); that's why being a Catholic was harder but finally better: you had to acknowledge that you were eating someone else's flesh. You had to live with that.

When the visiting priest left the hospital chapel—he put the black coat right over the alb and stole, not folding either this time—we five remained seated for his solitary procession down the center aisle. He had said the Mass alone, without a single altar boy.

After the others filed out, Nurse tapped me on the shoulder. "It's time," she whispered.

I put up a hand. "Five minutes." I made my way to the left of the altar to light a candle.

A wood-and-vinyl prayer stand knelt before twelve red candles that were arranged in an elaborate metal holder. I lowered myself and ducked my head, pretending to pray. After a minute, I peeked beneath my armpit. Nurse had ensconced herself in the first row, arms folded against her bibbed chest, legs crossed. The overalls hiked up an inch, and I could see her fallen knee-highs and a stripe of peach skin.

I went back to the candles. A clump of long wooden sticks rested on a corner of the candle rack. I dipped one into the nearest flame and lit an untried wick. I looked up. Smelled the silky wax. The cross was very ordinary, hand-painted plaster on wood. Sort of stock crucifixion, which sounded like an oxymoron: how could such agony become generic? But it had, the true beauty of his sacrifice disguised by the too sad eyes and the artificial expression of regret and pain. I counted his ribs, I always did; there were thirteen.

Christ was the first anorexic. Most people don't realize, but it's true.

I could hear the soft squidge of Nurse's rubber-soled shoes. She stood behind me.

"It's time," she whispered to the back of my head. "They said you had to return by ten at the absolute latest. It's five of."

Still kneeling, I turned around. "The lilies stink," I said. "Pee-you." I wrinkled my nose, but Nurse didn't laugh. "They're for Easter, you know."

"Come on. Gert said you couldn't ever come again if you got back late. Just this first time you have to do it exactly right."

"Lilies and chocolate. That's what Easter means to them. Disgusting."

"I'll get in trouble if you're not back in time."

"Most people don't have a clue as to what Easter is about."

Nurse sighed.

"What they don't understand is that the miracle wasn't in the Resurrection. The miracle was in his complete denial of self."

"Just the same," she said, "it's time to go."

I stood up stiffly. My knees felt as if they had cracked in half. Pain skimmed along the bone until it gained my hip. I couldn't remember if I had ever knelt at this particular weight—ninety-four was it?—for this long. Nurse took my elbow and steered me down the aisle.

We picked up our palms by the door, sharp-edged reeds, square and thickish at one end, slender and pointed at the other. Nurse gave me one. It felt cool between my fingers. I fanned her with the reed.

"Do you know what it means, the Passion of Christ?"

She shook her head.

"It means the suffering of Christ. In Latin, *suffering* and *passion* come from the same root word."

"I didn't know that."

"Historically it refers to his final days, from about the Last Supper to when he was buried. But I've always sort of thought of it as starting with Palm Sunday, the day he rode into town and was hailed as a king. They fanned him with palms." I ruffled my palm at Nurse again, and she picked up a second one from the table. She turned them over in her hands.

"Five days later, on Good Friday, he was dead. The thing was, he knew when he first got there, when they were treating him so nice, that the same people would hand him over to be killed by the end of the week. That was the suffering part. The knowing."

We walked out of the chapel and over to the wide automatic glass doors. It was misting out—a sheet of dampness instead of rain in measured droplets. Spring was five days old. Nurse waved good-bye until I was out of sight. It did not feel like renewal to me. I would be chilled all day.

PART

II

Seven

Everyone on our unit got dressed up for the mixed Twelve Step meeting on Friday night. All the patients from all the floors went. It was the only time we were allowed to see the others.

We had an hour after dinner before going down to the lecture hall. The nurse on duty unlocked the central cabinet where razors were kept. We took off our pants and socks and stood in line waiting for the shower stall, where the nurse supervised our shaving. The line went halfway down the hall. She held back the shower curtain and made us go in three at a time, our fannies touching when we bent to shave. The showerhead detached, and she held it herself, inspecting our careful strokes, then spraying off the shaving cream, looking for cuts. The anorexics went last because we took the longest; when you get that thin, your body grows more hair to keep you warm. Gwen went twice, once with me and Amy, and once just with Louise because Louise couldn't bend. In the end, she was the only girl without ankle fringe because someone else had done it. Gwen had more hair than any of us.

After, we crammed into the same elevator, all seventeen girls, and rode down the single flight. The weight limit was three thousand pounds. I tried to do the math—for every one under a hundred pounds, there were two or three girls grossly overweight—but Janine was talking. Still teaching me things.

"We ride the elevator to the mixed meeting," she

said, "because it's like making an entrance. We could take the stairs, but we don't."

We entered the lecture hall—somewhat misnamed—it was a regular meeting room like the others, only twice the size—still smelling of Old Spice. But no one was there to receive our splendor. We began setting up chairs. The other units came ten minutes later, escorted by their counselors. We heard them before we saw them: their shuffling weight against the staircase, the unrestrained male voices. All the girls ran to a spot to sit or stand. Janine and two of the other bulimics waited by the entrance to greet the men, a garish welcome wagon. They had teased their hair and wore the same brick red lipstick; there must have been only one tube. The color was so dark that their lips stood away from their faces. When they talked, the lips moved like little erratic birds. The sluttiest one wore a fat, sixties-style belt that cinched her waist tight enough to pinken her face. Gwen and Amy fussed at the empty food cart in the back of the room, arranging the napkins in an elaborate fan. Queen Victoria sat in one of the middle rows with Louise, who was trying to hide two front strands of hair, which she'd singed with a curling iron. I'd brought a book and was pretending to read.

The lecture hall filled quickly; two of them for every one of us. A crowd gathered around the speaker's platform. So far, all the men we'd seen were doctors or nurses: wrinkly, scrubbed, and condescending. These men were bigger and more lethargic; they laughed but they did not smile. Some were in terrible shape—the ones still going through detox. They wore hospital whites and slippers, and when you looked in their eyes, you could tell they couldn't focus. Actually, all the men wore slippers—Seaview slippers with a seahorse stitched on the big toe. The new arrivals had little makeup bags as well. I watched a man with a shaved head examine his. It was an amenities kit, like what you get when you fly first-class. Syd loved these, the little blindfolds especially. Seaview's version was more mundane: soap, hand cream, shampoo, toothpaste, and toothbrush. I wondered why they got so many extras.

There were a few women in their group, but we hardly noticed them. They were skinny in a furtive, unintentional way, unlike any of us. They were smokers who looked down at the floor and picked at their cuticles until they bled. One of them, the smallest person I had ever seen who was not a dwarf, had tattoos covering both arms. Her name was Tiny Regular.

When a counselor called the meeting to order, everyone still standing went for seats. I ended up next to Janine and her slutty friends; Louise, Queen Victoria, Gwen, and Amy sat in the next row. The men spread out around us, the recent arrivals sitting farthest back.

The meeting was like and unlike our Overeaters Anonymous meetings, which we attended every night except this one. The rhythm was the same, but the text was distinct. Gert had said they mixed us together on Friday nights so we could widen our perspectives. "So you can see the disease in its various, insidious forms," she'd said.

That night, a cocaine addict identified as Joey R. told his story. He started with his freaking wife, then went on to losing his freaking job, and selling toot to keep up with the freaking Joneses. His story ended with the freaking cops.

"In closing," he said, "I'd just like to say that with the help of a Higher Power, I am taking it One Day at a Time and living without the freaking blow. If I can do it, you can do it too."

I felt like I was at the movies. He never once said the word *cocaine*. When he was through sharing, Joey R. called on his friends.

All the men talked this way, using a series of slogans in specific sequence. It was like a code. They each said how grateful they were. It appeared to be against the rules *not* to be grateful. The slogans seemed elaborate, gentle rationalizations for failure. For wanting, then accepting less. Easy Does

It. First Things First. Live and Let Live. It didn't matter what they couldn't do anymore. It was all okay.

I noticed there was a hierarchy of addiction. The worse your story, the more profound your degradation, the more revered your recovery, the more slaps on the back you received after the meeting. Which left us in a funny predicament. Us, as in we, the girls. We had not lost jobs or wives or houses. For the most part we did not have things to lose; we were part of what other people lost. Fat or emaciated, average-looking but obsessed, garbage pickers and pukers, we lived in houses that we did not pay for, houses with convection ovens and Cuisinarts, juicers and microwaves. None of us shared at the big mixed meeting.

Earlier, Gert had said, "Listen for what you identify with, not for what makes you different." But it was difference that was compelling. Romantic at first, repulsive in time.

They were working-class mostly. A mix of races. Laborers and postmen. Muscular or potbellied or tattooed. We were all white and three-quarters college-educated. There were exceptions, but not enough to matter. The men were poorer and more dangerous. When we left Seaview, we would talk about them, these once-a-week meetings, these glimpsed lives. Not each other, not ourselves. Not food.

Listening to the others, we felt ashamed caring as much as we did about food. We felt frivolous.

Maybe this, in the end, was the plan.

When everyone who'd wanted to had shared, the night-shift counselors made us hold hands and say a prayer. I thought of the Charismatic Catholics—the ones who stood through Mass with their hands out to their sides, waiting to feel God tickle their palms—as I looked around the circle. People's eyes were shut tight.

Immediately after, the counselors stocked the food cart with fruit, apples, oranges, pears, and herbal tea, our evening snack. When everything was set out, a legion of men with first names and last initials, and even the taciturn Tiny

Regular, complained about the absence of cookies and coffee, which they said were always provided at their meetings. Food, for obvious reasons, was not allowed during ours, and it was in deference to us that the administration excluded caffeine and sugar from the mixed meeting.

Joey R. spoke for all the addicts when he went up to one of the counselors, and said angrily, "Where are the Entenmann's? Where are the Chips Ahoy!?" He slammed his folding chair and cursed loud enough for us to hear.

"They do this every week," said Janine, her face and neck damp with sweat. During the prayer, she'd stood between Joey R. and a man still detoxing.

Even I could tell it was false outrage. The men were glad to have us, compelled as much by our difference as we were by theirs. We were women after all.

During the hour of informal chat that followed the meeting, the bulimics were, without question, the most indiscreet. They reached around bodies at the fruit cart, their breasts brushing against shoulders as they strained for pears. The drug addicts were genuinely friendly, hugging everyone instead of shaking hands. They called each other "family." As time passed, the talk grew low, provocative. Questions were personal; the meeting had created a certain intimacy.

Queen Victoria said to a group of women and men, "I've had a lifelong affair with a woman, and I'm not ashamed to admit it. Her name: Sara Lee."

There were snickers, laughter, more reaching for fruit.

Amy, Gwen, and I lurked at the edges of the room, experts in not wanting. The compulsive overeaters eavesdropped, hanging on the lip of others' conversations or in a cluster around a man who had somehow indicated his preference for bigger women. Louise kept fooling with the strands of hair she had burned with the curling iron.

Even these private conversations had the same funny cadence as the meeting. I guessed this was the ticket out of Seaview: surrendering all of what was mine including—

maybe especially—the way I spoke. It was George Orwell, not Jim Jones, they'd borrowed from.

At ten, the counselors shooed us away. We girls had to leave first, so as not to see the men get counted. This humiliated them, and they had asked that we never see them queuing up for counting. They took the elevators back home. Already on our unit, I heard the ping and hum of the machinery as they passed. Few girls were up on our floor. Most everyone had gone straight to bed.

Friday nights, after the mixed meeting, the bulimics skipped their regular bedtime ablutions, hoping to finish masturbating before their anorexic or overeating roommates returned from the bathroom. If they didn't finish in time, they would have had to wait until their roommates fell asleep. And who knew whether the roommates themselves wouldn't have been listening, impatient, for the sound of regular breathing across the two-foot divide between beds? Fortunate were those who could do it standing up, in a bathroom stall, without losing balance when they came. Or the girls who could straddle the toilet, ignoring vulgar associations. All this before the nurse with her foot in the door took notice. Not that I knew from experience. Janine had told me.

My senior year in high school, I had sex with my best friend Ronald. It was both of our first times. Except that he at least had touched himself before. Ronald was even more Catholic than I. More devout. I knew because we had gone to church and had been confirmed together. I'd seen his faith: delicate fingers fondling black beads, peach lips loosed around one Our Father for every ten Hail Marys. "As if divinity could be expressed exponentially," he'd said, "and Mary were divine by one-tenth the power."

But at seventeen I hadn't yet explored myself, and Ronald had. I agreed to sex partly because I knew Syd dreaded it—Ronald was black—but mostly because I couldn't imagine trusting anyone as much as I trusted him.

During our first (and only) time together, he asked, "Don't you ever do this, touch yourself this way?"

Eight

Syd brought my swimming gear so I could use the pool. I gave her a tour of the first two floors. I introduced her. She thought the rooms were dismal, the girls strange. I brought her to see the athletic facilities. When we reached the pool, her nose curled pleasantly at the chlorine. She took a deep breath. I had mentioned, let it slip, the business about a single room.

"And why does that little girl have her own room? Does anyone say?" Syd stepped carefully on the alabaster tile. Her fat-heeled pumps slid a little, but she did not lose her balance. Her short skirt showed off her good legs. She'd been a synchronized swimmer in college.

"I don't know."

"Is there a reason? Does she have a problem, or was it just the luck of the draw, she came in when there was a single available?"

"Syd, everyone here has a problem."

"Don't get smart with me."

I was pretending not to care. I was pretending her interest embarrassed me. I knew from practice that this would egg her on.

"What I mean is, does she have another problem, one that makes her incapable of having a roommate?" Syd picked up a Styrofoam kickboard from a pile by the edge of the pool. Aquamarine seahorses swam on either side. "Is she terribly antisocial?"

"Oh, I don't know. She's a child actor or something. So she says. Maybe she's used to her own dressing room. Maybe her mother called to complain. Maybe she's just a brat."

"Well, it is small. You were right about that." She was talking about the pool now. She bent down and set the kickboard afloat. The water was blue-white. She dipped a finger into the chlorine and brought it to her lips and nose. "Whew, way overdone." She rose and straightened her skirt. "Better to err on the side of caution, I suppose, but still. Be sure to wear your cap when you go in."

When we left the pool, she met with my private shrink, Dana. I waited in my room. Janine had left for the mall. After ten days at Seaview, patients were allowed to go, in a group, to the nearby mall in Hanover. Syd and I had shopped there. It was upscale. A Lord and Taylor and no Sears.

There was nothing for me to do in my room. I put away the swimsuit, cap, goggles, and earplugs. I had fancy earplugs called ear molds, not the regular, mini sink stoppers most people buy at the pharmacy. So did Syd. We both had bad ears from swimming.

I'd been swimming from practically the day I was born. Syd took me to underwater infant classes at the YMCA. Nobody belonged to the Y in those days; it was before aerobics and weightlifting. Only a few people went. Syd said mostly old-timers. She swam twice a week in the green-and-yellow-tiled pool with a mosaic of Neptune (one of the spears of his trident was missing) inset along the floor. When *Life* magazine did a story on newborns who were dropped into pools and knew instantly to hold their breaths, the Y began to offer infant classes. In her sixth month of pregnancy, before she had even decided on my name, Syd enrolled us.

The underwater infant swimming was a method, like the Lamaze method, natural and radical and supposedly nurturing to the mother-child bond. Syd was excited about mothering at first, before she had two of us so small. I could picture her at the Y in 1959, her swimmer's figure outshining all the other mothers, her rose-colored bathing cap matching her black and pink suit. She was by far the best swimmer in the class, the only mom with the proper relationship to the water, according to the instructor.

"Ladies, ladies!" he scolded. "How will your child learn to be at home in the water, if you, yourselves, are not?"

Syd said the other mothers avoided her. She thought they disapproved of her close-fitting suit. It was a racing suit that did not end in a skirt, like theirs, but ended high up on her leg, showing smooth, muscular thighs. I bet they coveted her cinched waist and flat stomach that made no reference to childbirth. I bet they hated her nonchalance in the water, her flirtatious rapport with Sven, the instructor, who came all the way from Sweden to spread underwater infant swimming throughout the United States. But the ladies did not hate me.

Syd said I was a lousy swimmer at three months. The first few weeks, I screamed at the dip of a toe. The other mothers smiled and cooed at me, charmed by my hysteria, my tight red fists and contorted face. But Syd persisted. She knew I had to inherit something from her, and she willed it to be her love of the water: its cool rush against her shoulder blades, the shapes it made between her calves during underwater arabesques, the stillness way far down, the weightlessness. She lowered me an inch at a time into the chlorinated pool. By the fourth week, I had mastered my terror. The other mothers stood still and envious, infants propped on their hips-made-shelves, as Syd and I swam in tandem along the floor of the shallow end. Their veiny thighs must have looked like underwater trees to us, rooted in the tile. Each week we followed the long spear of Neptune across the bottom of the pool, our cheeks ballooned with air, my fist around Syd's giant thumb.

"That Dale is so extreme-looking." Syd was at my door. "I don't know how you can confide in someone like that. If she just grew her hair, it would help a thousand times."

"It's Dana, not Dale. Her name is Dana. What did she have to say?"

Syd crossed to the edge of my bed. "You could only be moved in the event of an emergency, and she saw no emergency."

"Thanks for asking, Syd, really."

"Well, I'm not through. I've got the name of her boss and I'm calling him on Monday. For what I'm paying for this place, you should at least have some privacy."

"Did she say anything about Amy? Why she had a single?"

Syd shook her head. "She absolutely refused to talk about it. To tell you the truth, Dale wasn't particularly forthcoming. All she was interested in was some sort of public family therapy. I told her absolutely not."

It was a funny picture, Syd with Dana.

"I always imagined therapists as soft touches," she said. "Chronic givers. But not that one. Not that Dale."

I said, "It's part of their job to be like that. To be objective."

"It surprised me, that's all. How cold she was," said Syd. "Matter-of-fact. As if your being here could be matter-of-fact."

"I'm sure it is to her."

"Well, it's not to me."

We had a ritual of contrariness, my mother and I; we were compelled to say opposing things even when what we wanted was the same.

"It couldn't be less matter-of-fact to me." Her voice quavered. For a moment, I thought she was going to cry. But she steeled herself.

"We'll see about the move," she said. "I'm not finished yet."

And she wasn't.

Nine

The next morning, I refused to get up for meditation. I told them I wasn't feeling well and needed to sleep late, but promised to make breakfast. Then I spent the morning *in the mirror*, which was an old expression of Syd's. "Get out of the mirror," she used to holler when I spent all my time there. Of course, I'd gotten it from her.

The shrinks encouraged us to look "frankly" at our naked bodies at least once a day. Roommates were supposed to honor requests for a few minutes of private time. A long, rectangular mirror hung on the back of every patient room door. As soon as Janine left, I shut our door and propped a chair against it.

I took off my clothes and stood close to the glass. I was thinking what I always think: wouldn't it be nice to be truly in the mirror, like the other, fictive Alice, two-dimensional instead of three? The appearance of life without the mess.

My skin was almost gray. Black Irish, like my grandmother Grace, Syd's mother, with black hair and white, white skin, no freckles. Skin so white it's bluish sometimes, transparent others. But not this morning. I leaned forward until my nipples touched the glass. The skin around them bunched up tight like closing flowers. Montgomery glands, that's what they're called, those ugly little bumps surrounding the nipple. When they do breast reductions, they cut out around your montgomery glands, and lift them off, like the top of a cookie jar. Then they suck out the fat and sew them back on. I tried to picture that, tracing my finger around the edge of my areolas and then pulling on my nipples until they changed from blue to red. They said about eighty percent of the women who have it done lose some sensation.

It was not that mine were very big. I had not become anorexic because mine got unmanageably big. Besides, that was their paradigm. They thought my anorexia was a reaction to some event in my past. With all their education and experience, they didn't seem to realize it was more complicated.

What was my body like before, they wanted to know. Dana said adolescents often developed anorexia to keep from getting women's bodies.

"Like Amy?"

She wouldn't answer.

I had had a certain pudginess growing up. Not a fat kid. Nothing teasable. But it stayed with me. I went on my first diet in the seventh grade. Syd and I together. A fruit diet. Three squares: grapefruit, banana, watermelon. I discovered that even thin, I didn't like my body. It never looked right. I was too wide across, so the curves seemed boxy. The breasts weren't fruit-shaped, they were pointed, the nipples aiming down, the right one a whole cup-size larger than the left. The rest belonged to my father: long legs, no rear, short waist. It was an enormous disappointment to realize dieting wouldn't give me Syd's body. I stopped then, when I got to high school, when most of the girls were going wild with it: Stillman, Scarsdale, high-protein, low-protein, steak-lovers, grapefruit, etc. I just resigned myself.

The thing about great bodies was you either had one or you didn't. So much of life was like that. Beauty, smarts, athletic ability—all givens. Dad believed in working hard, training to get ahead. Before he became a lawyer, he played tennis, right on that line between professional and amateur. He'd had a weak serve, he said, that's what killed his game. But he tried. Syd said he practiced four hours a day while going to law school. He had even had two different coaches.

When they ran out of money, he gave it up. In those days, wives didn't work.

I figured the experience would have made him come down harder on the genetic-advantage side of things. But it didn't. He was an American Wayer: work, work, work, and you shall receive. When I asked him about it, he said he'd have hated himself if he didn't try, but that he was smart enough to have had something to fall back on.

It seemed to me that was what sunk him. After all, what were fallbacks, if not a lack of faith? People knew the truth about themselves. Who they were. What they could do.

In every swim meet I ever lost, I knew who'd beat me from the moment I left the slippery tile floor for the textured starting block. It was the way she shook out her muscles, the long limbs rippling, redundant, like pool water; the way she bent over and grabbed beneath the block to stretch her hamstrings; the way she snapped her cap in place. All these things told me. We either win or lose.

It was a lot to know. Right there, on the starting blocks, the glands in my neck would swell. My eustachian tubes, the dark, slender passageways from throat to ears, throbbed. A lot came with it: the Why bothers? Why get up in the morning when I already knew? Why try? So much of my life seemed already finished.

Syd never had that. Possibility was everywhere for her. Even after her big disappointment, after my father left. She had the body for possibility, the face for excitement. Anything could happen. All she had to do was look in the mirror to know that every book ever written, every movie, every song, could have been about her. My mother could insert herself anywhere.

If I had had to say my anorexia was about any single thing, I would have said it was about living without desire. Without longing of any kind.

In the mirror, I looked more or less the same. Which was what I worked toward, no surprises. My breasts were like my Grandma Grace's breasts before she died, between raisins and prunes. To tell the truth, men's fascination with breasts always embarrassed me, especially when one would suck on mine. Though only one ever did, Ronald. It happened before my breasts disappeared. And once with my little brother, Alex, which I never counted. We were seven and six years old and I made him; it was something we'd seen on late-night TV after my parents' light had disappeared from under their door and we'd snuck into the living room. But even with Ronald, my closest friend, I had thought of animals when he put his mouth on my breasts. I smelled milk.

I was in high school when I realized I would never be beautiful; before I had realized *I wasn't*, but in high school it dawned that *I'd never be*. I pretended faith, then intellect, were the things I truly valued. Nothing so superficial as appearance. I looked down my nose at girls who fussed. But with time came the suffocating recognition of what I'd lost.

The irony was that so many anorexics were exquisite. Gwen was model-pretty, a Ralph Lauren dream of wholesomeness. Even little Amy had a chiseled look. You got the impression they were starving themselves for protection— they got so much scrutiny from the outside world. I was the anomaly: an average anorexic. Mundane in all things. Even aberration.

Ten

———

hey made us all floss our teeth. Publicly, in front of the counselors and nurses. A dentist delivered the general lecture. He showed slides of rotting teeth and inflamed gums, close-up shots that looked like the insides of damp caves. Gert worked the rickety projector, which was set up in the group room. He talked specifically about the dental problems of people with eating disorders. He said he could tell the moment a patient opened her mouth whether she overate or underate or purged. No one believed him at first, until he started talking about stomach acid eating the enamel off the bulimic girls' teeth.

"Not the back," he said, smiling in the dusk, showing us the inky gap between his own front teeth, "unless purging has been sustained over several years. Then both the front and back are affected."

When the lights came up after the slides, the guest dentist put on yellow surgical gloves and instructed the nurses to hand out mirrors and floss to each of us. He was very handsome, tall and broad-chested, with reddish brown skin and sun-bleached blond hair that fell across his eyes. An outdoorsman, like Alex. Probably white water rafting or sculling on the Charles River. He hadn't worn a tee shirt under his white button-down, and his minuscule nipples poked like pen tips through the expensive cloth.

"Of course, overeaters often have more cavities than one can count, sometimes two or three per tooth," he said. "Undereaters can be the hardest to diagnose. Their mouths suffer from malnutrition, like the rest of their bodies. Eventually, gum disease sets in and their teeth come away from the bone and fall out." He wrapped a long piece of floss around the middle finger of each gloved hand and held it up to demonstrate, quite pleased with himself, like an older girl doing cat's cradle.

The mirrors were small and round with wire stands so that we could set them on the long conference table that was brought in especially for his lecture. One side of the mirror showed a regular reflection; the other side showed it magnified several times. I flipped to the magnified side. My face leapt toward me, exaggerated and out of focus, wobbly in the glass. My amplified image would not hold still.

"Make sure you curve the thread around the shape of the tooth and gently move beneath the gum line."

Louise and Gwen tried to help each other find the right angle of floss to tooth. Louise worked with her hands too deep in her mouth, three or four fingers around each tooth; Gwen worked with her hands way out by the side of her head. The guest dentist squatted next to them and demonstrated on his own molars.

When the lecture was over, we were allowed to keep the floss, bright plastic hexagons stuffed with the silk-white thread. But the dentist took back the mirrors, collecting them in a burlap sack. "For next time." He smiled. The gap between his two front teeth made him stunning rather than simply handsome; it was the kind of imperfection that unified the whole. He was probably very photogenic.

I had the urge to trip him as he went out the door. The image of him sprawled like a cat on all fours, surrounded by shards of broken glass, popped into view like one of his slides.

Eleven

I wondered whether acting bad or acting good would get me a single room at Seaview. I knew they already thought I had a bad attitude. Which was unusual. I was used to being perceived as having a good attitude. Self-control, self-effacement, self-denial. People like this, especially in girls. But there was a line. As in all things, the point where you separated yourself from other people. Whenever I made a scene growing up, a tantrum or a public talking-back, Syd would say, "You're crossing the line now." As if she could see it there, painted on the floor.

I tried to take my cue from Amy, but she wasn't much help. In the first place, she had a different schedule. No art therapy, no exercise, only half as much group. She came to meditation, to all our Twelve Step stuff, to meals. Apparently she got lots of individual. And then, when she was around, she was quiet. If you engaged her in any way, she told you about her acting career, which no one but Gwen believed in. She mentioned commercials, off-off-Broadway, summer stock. Even Janine, Pollyanna, nice-to-everyone-because-I'm-getting-out-of-here Janine, said, "How many productions of *Annie* can there be in the world?"

Amy did have an actor's voice, deep and sometimes raspy. If you closed your eyes while she spoke, you'd think it was a woman in her twenties, not a thirteen-year-old kid; when you opened them again, there was Amy, looking ten. I didn't do that more than once. She complained about sore throats and they allowed her special herbal lozenges that she was always sucking.

Likely, my best shot at a private room was acting bad. If goody two-shoes Janine hadn't been awarded a single room, it was doubtful I would be, especially given my already deleterious attitude. The difficulty lay in not acting so bad that it would prolong my stay. Which seemed to be what had happened to Amy.

Still, I mostly counted on Syd. She had promised to meet with the director and she was used to getting her way.

I was up to ninety-eight pounds. My team okayed me for exercise. The gym was hardly state-of-the-art, four poorly ventilated rooms, interconnecting. Mary Beth handed me an index card with "Individualized Fitness Plan" printed across the top. I remembered reading about this in the Seaview brochure: "We will provide your daughter with an Individualized Fitness Plan." Mine said I was not allowed aerobic exercise nor the use of heavy weights. All I could do was stretch and swim.

Mary Beth shook my hand as if we'd made a deal. "I hope you use the pool. I hear you're quite the fish."

"You call that a pool?"

"Just remember," Mary Beth said. "No laps."

The exercise room had a padded floor and mirrors along one wall. Girls sat on white terry towels, stretching. I found Janine and sat beside her. My card said I was allowed to do the warm-up and warm-down parts of the aerobic routine. During the middle, the fifteen minutes of intense workout, I was supposed to breathe deeply and stretch.

Like Cass, Mary Beth divided us up by disorder: compulsive eaters to the left, anorexics on the right, bulimics up the middle. She said she needed a floor plan that made clear who was allowed to do what. We'd pretty much arranged ourselves that way anyway. The bulimics had all different kinds of bodies, some "normal," some fat, some muscular. More voluptuous than not. They helped us make the transition, visually at least, between the extremes.

"What's her story," I asked Janine.

"Who?"

I looked at our instructor. Mary Beth was explaining to Louise why she couldn't put her towel next to Gwen's. Each muscle in Mary Beth's arms and legs stood out from the others, like the parts of a braid.

"She used to exercise at a very swank gym in New York City," said Janine. "Stars went there. John Travolta and Bette Midler and Sly Stallone. Mary Beth exercised for two and a half hours after every meal, eventually after every bite. She never left the health club, she didn't have to; there was a juice bar and a café inside. She couldn't keep a job. She put it all on Visa."

"She charged it?"

Just then Mary Beth asked for our attention. She stood facing us with her back to the mirror. I could see firm buttocks in the glass. "I want everyone to take a deep breath." She popped a cassette into a tape player. New Age crap. I couldn't even name the instruments.

"Feel your muscles contract and reelaaax," she said, "contract and reelaaax. Make peace with your body. It is exactly as it's supposed to be at this moment."

Mary Beth wore bicycle shorts and a ripped-up tee shirt. Her muscles showed through. The music got faster, more familiar. People grunted. Six of us were restricted from full participation; we sat stretching. I had already decided this was not how I was going to misbehave. I hated aerobics anyway; usually only the instructor and her acolytes managed not to look asinine. One of the girls, an exercise bulimic named Penny, was clearly in distress. Halfway into the routine, she stood up and began to bounce in place to the music. Mary Beth glared at her until she bounced back down.

Penny was famous throughout Seaview. Even the drug addicts talked about her. She'd gone AWOL on her first day. But instead of really leaving, she'd run in a six-mile loop around the hospital grounds. This was what the addicts marveled at, that she hadn't gone to cop. What they didn't realize was that for Penny there wasn't a place to cop; she could do it anywhere. Gert drove by her on the way home from work that day. Penny had started a second loop when Gert pulled up and offered her a lift. She was running in blue jeans and oxford shoes. A doctor from Medical was called in to treat the blisters.

By the end of the workout, Mary Beth's clothes looked smaller. Her skin was brown and wet, pulled tight like plastic wrap. She said, "Close your eyes and concentrate on the muscles you will need to lift your leg. Picture them contracting."

She was pretty Zen for an aerobics instructor, I had to admit. Mercifully not perky.

The locker room had an open shower. We weren't forced to use it. We could have gone upstairs to the more-or-less private showers on our floor if we wanted. Most girls did. Only the exercise bulimics showered downstairs. Penny and two others crowded under the available showerheads and soaped themselves. In order to stay warm under the separate sprays, they had to move back and forth in a kind of figure eight, their elbows brushing. I watched them from the lockers, only a few feet away, where I pretended to towel dry. They posed for each other by dropping the soap or by reaching for difficult spots with a washcloth. Naked, their bodies were odd: flat and bulbous at once, inflated here, concave there. The shower water ran in funny streams along their frames, never just straight down, around quadriceps and triceps, trapeziuses and deltoids, diverted first by one, then by a second muscle group. They looked like malformed toys to me. But apparently not to them. I wondered what they saw as they contorted themselves in the shower, revealing hidden muscles for one another's admiration.

Their clothes lay in three neat piles on the worn bench closest to the showers. What caught my eye was a powder blue sanitary napkin sticking out of one of the piles; someone had her period. I wondered who. Exercise bulimics lost their periods almost as often as we did: twenty percent body fat was necessary in order to bleed. I knew because I began skipping mine during freshman year in college, about the time of my falling out with Ronald. What was funny was that Syd had had a very early menopause—premature ovarian failure they called it; she was forty-two—and we stopped bleeding at the same time. I remembered because she went to lots of doctors.

The napkin was the adhesive variety, something I'd hardly worn. In the last few years, the technology had changed. No more belts. Syd had shown me how to wear one, demonstrating on herself in front of a mirror. We practiced threading the little flaps through the metal part and hooking them on the sharp teeth. Syd explained that the belt was supposed to ride low, like hip-huggers. The metal dug into my soft skin and pulled at my pubic hair. I had wanted to scratch. Syd said it was a shame my pubic hair was so dark. She raised her arms and lifted her shirt so I could see the curve of her waist and flat belly.

"Not bad for an old lady?"

Syd's pubic hair was light, not exactly blond like the hair on her head, but lighter than mine. And she had a lot more of it than me. A tiny blondish afro. I thought of an expression I had heard at school but hadn't, until then, understood. In the cafeteria, boys would ask the lunchroom ladies if there was any fur pie for dessert and then crack up. I wondered if Alex knew about fur pie.

The girls in the shower were too busy admiring themselves to notice me hovering around their things. Here was my opportunity. I would get in trouble for this. Bad enough trouble, I hoped, for a single room. I picked up their clothes and ran.

Twelve

When the screaming started, I was in the stairwell, not even halfway to the second floor. I was on tip-toe, trying to minimize the slap of my loafers against the steel-lined steps, my body hunched around the ball of purloined towels and clothes, when I heard the first ecstatic peal. I froze.

Their voices trilled. "Where are our clothes? Where are our clothes? We have nothing to wear!"

I took the remaining stairs two at a time and ditched the wad of clothes in the first plastic laundry basket I found on our hall, the kind the orderlies emptied twice a day. I went straight to my room.

What happened next, I heard that night at dinner. Amy got the story from the nurses. She'd been here so long they'd relaxed their standards. According to Amy, when Mary Beth went for towels and robes she told the exercise bulimics in no uncertain terms to stay put. Penny and her two friends (one a squat bodybuilder who'd done so many steroids she'd grown a black mustache, plus a former Ironwoman triathlete who wore her medal every day beneath her clothes) said, Of course. Where could we possibly go like this?

As soon as Mary Beth left, they skipped from the lockers to the dinky pool, to the exercise room where we'd aerobicized together, to the torture-chamber weight room at the farthest end. Naked. Brazen under full fluorescent lights. They calculated: Mary Beth would be gone eight to twelve minutes. Time enough. Because the doors to all four airless gym rooms had no locks, the girls squandered some precious, unsupervised minutes wandering back and forth, considering. A swim? Laps? An underwater race? Six sets of bench-presses? But then Penny noticed the tape sitting silently in the cassette player where Mary Beth had left it, and that was that. She flipped the side. Fast-forwarded until she found the disco, then punched play.

Penny was a professional dancer turned aerobics instructor. In group therapy, she'd said to us, "Who cared, after a while, what the movement meant? What the dance was saying?"

She began a favorite routine, fitting her prearranged steps into the music. The others followed, each a full arm's length away from Penny, each with an unobstructed view of herself in the mirror.

They watched themselves dance.

That's how Mary Beth found them when she got back. Deaf to her shouts. The music blasting. Their bodies gleaming. Hard. Jiggle-free. Sculptures of flesh, bouncing up and down like playground balls, seamless. As if each girl had been formed from a liquid mold.

Mary Beth yanked the tape. It took a minute for them to stop. The music rang in their ears. They unwound, a backward-spinning spiral.

When everything got still, Penny screamed.

We didn't see them again until the following day at breakfast. They'd been shuffled off to their individual shrinks and to team meetings. At breakfast, we saved them seats and shared our most-esteemed food item, fresh-squeezed orange juice. Louise even carried their empty trays back to the serving window, making three separate trips.

Thirteen

———

Before lunch, I was called to a meeting with my team in Dana's office. Gert, Cass, Mary Beth, Dana, and my admitting physician, Dr. Paul, sat in a circle with their knees clamped together. There was one empty chair. Gert patted it, directing me to sit. Dana did the talking.

"We'd like to discuss the shower incident," she said.

Not theft. Not misconduct. Not prank. *The shower incident.* I thought, Here comes that ineffable Seaview sense of humor.

She said, "Do you enjoy watching people?"

"Depends on what they're doing."

"Do you feel more powerful when you can see someone, but they can't see you?"

"Not necessarily."

"Do you enjoy watching women in particular?"

It was more than I'd bargained for. I didn't say anything for a full minute.

Being mostly therapists, they waited.

The truth was, I did like to watch people and I did like to watch women in particular, but not for the reasons they thought. Anorexics are observers, measurers. We spectate other lives, other choices. I watched women's bodies, not for pleasure, but with the hope of finding imperfection.

Dana cleared her throat. "Your mother met with the director last Friday. And then with Dr. Sampson."

Dr. Paul leafed through my file with his pudgy hands.

"Mrs. Forrester feels strongly about you having your own room," said Dana. "She made a compelling case for it."

I tried to read Dana's face. Did she hate my mother? I wondered if Syd had said anything belittling about her to the director.

"Dr. Sampson, I believe, concurs."

He nodded without looking up, his nose still in my file. As if he were looking for something instead of just hiding out.

"We were reluctant at first." She glanced at the others. "But now, with Janine leaving Friday, we think we've found a way. You and Amy will switch rooms when Janine moves out. Amy and a new girl will be roommates. We think it will benefit Amy as well. The company. You'll be by yourself."

It felt strange to get a room this way. I hadn't thought about the conclusions they would draw. My stomach fluttered. What would they tell the others? Not to shower with Alice?

"And there's one other thing. We've called a moratorium on your mother."

"A what?"

"We think a separation will facilitate your recovery."

"She can't visit anymore?"

"The mother-daughter bond can be the most intense relationship in a woman's life."

"Especially for a single woman," said Dr. Paul.

Fourteen

At Janine's parting ritual, her chair broke. It was simply a going-away party, but they called it a parting ritual because they thought themselves deeply spiritual. They were not so good at throwing parties at Seaview; they had nothing to serve and insensibly forbade streamers and balloons. Instead, we decorated the group room with twice as many posters and plaques than was usual. Both primary groups (we split in two for group therapy; seventeen was too many for psychic delving) were present. Each girl brought what was in her room, and the counselors donated things from their offices and homes. I had never seen so many embroidered Serenity Prayers assembled in one place. Cass hung Janine's giant body drawing on the wall for everyone to see. At the opposite end of the room, a lopsided card table supported apple juice and paper cups.

Gert and Dana led the ritual. They presented Janine with a copper-colored medallion with "One Day at a Time" written on one side and her name and the date inscribed on the other. It was bigger than a half dollar. The Seaview seahorse, tiny and imperfectly realized—it looked like a dog with wings—swum above Janine's name. If we didn't last the full stay, as prescribed by our doctors, we didn't get medallions. Which certainly sounded like the end of the world to me. Gert and Dana made each of us give Janine a symbolic gift.

"Something from your selves, your best selves, that you think Janine should have in the real world," said Gert.

Janine sat at the front of the room, her hands folded in her lap, her ankles crossed under the chair. She wore a white cotton dress that drooped in giant handkerchief points. Someone had placed a sprig of baby's breath behind her left ear. Gert and Dana stood on either side.

"I'll go first," said Dana.

The counselors always volunteered for each other's exercises. It was a trick of their trade. They thought enthusiasm was contagious.

"I give Janine the courage to have her feelings." Dana bent over and kissed Janine's cheek.

"I give Janine humility, or in other words, self-knowledge," said Gert, who also delivered a kiss.

It reminded me of the end of *The Wizard of Oz:* a heart, a brain, a home. We rose from our chairs and lined up before Janine.

"Serenity," said Queen Victoria.

"Hope," said Penny.

I was last in line.

"Self-love," said someone from the other primary group.

This was the worst so far. I had been at Seaview two weeks, a lifetime already, but not long enough to get accustomed to this sort of emotional extravagance.

"Happiness," said Penny's friend, the mustachioed bulimic.

The line began to dwindle.

"Peace."

"Faith."

I wanted to give Janine what the wizard gave Dorothy: absolutely nothing.

"Fellowship," said Louise, who was crying, of course.

"Joy," said Amy.

More than nothing: the absence of things, which was better. Desirelessness I wanted to give Janine. I was running out of time.

"Honesty."

"Understanding."

I tried to think of concrete gifts. The derriere she'd come in with, size-two jeans, a rowing machine.

"Serenity," said Gwen in a whisper, not realizing it was a gift already given.

Dana informed her.

Gwen looked stricken. She shrugged, and her white-blond hair almost came undone. I was next in line. If I blew on it, Gwen's hair would go. At last she thought of something: "Acceptance." She ducked down for the kiss. The movement was enough; her French braid disintegrated. The knot of hair fell forward. When Gwen's hair reached Janine's rouged cheek, Janine's chair sagged inexplicably to one side, the back left leg buckling, almost bending like a knee. As though Gwen's feathery hair had tipped an invisible balance. Janine knew it instantly and jerked herself to the right, away from the surrendering leg. But it was too late. The right side swooned from the unexpected surge of weight and the entire chair collapsed.

To my surprise, Janine did not land on the floor. She caught herself and remained squatting in midair, ankles still crossed, while the chair folded beneath her. A miraculous save, I thought. Perhaps awkward as she stumbled forward into Gwen, but less so than it would have been had she fallen.

"Grace," I said finally, over Gwen's shoulder, to the top of Janine's head. Gert was the only one who heard my gift. She scowled at me and grabbed the offending chair with one hand, removing it from the room before anyone had a chance to wonder. The ritual was over.

"Damn chairs," grumbled Gert, back in the group. "I've asked for replacements. They're about a hundred years old."

We nodded politely at her fib.

Janine stood slumped to one side, two of her handkerchief points skimming the carpet. She eyed her baby's breath on the floor. Gert wrapped her matron's arms around Janine and squeezed. Dana picked up the baby's breath and repositioned it behind Janine's ear.

"Time for final good-byes," she said.

Gert and Dana made Janine stand before her body drawing to receive well-wishers. She smiled like a mother of the bride, exhausted, relieved, secretly disappointed, and sad. You could see in the body drawing that she had been thinner when she first arrived, but nobody said anything. Gert put on music, some of Mary Beth's recreational tapes, and a few of the girls started to dance. I sat in a chair—they had all been pushed against the wall—and stared at my cup of apple juice. I kept picturing Janine's near fall; it had been impressive, her reflex to save herself. Little Amy came over and asked me to dance. I said no. She shrugged, disappointed.

"Thanks, though."

She shrugged again, feigning indifference, her lower lip extended. They had not told her about the impending room change yet. I wondered if she would still want to dance with me when she knew. Penny joined us, and after a brief exchange, the two rushed onto the dance floor. They swayed to the Jackson Five. *Easy as one, two, three.* Penny twisted everything to the beat. She could isolate each muscle group. Hips, stomach, legs, and shoulders all could move independently. She danced double-time, two pumps to every beat of the music. Amy could hardly keep up.

In the back of the room, by the wobbly refreshment table, Queen Victoria was teaching Gwen to waltz. *One, two, three*, but different. They watched their feet box on the carpet, neither of them listening to the Jackson Five. Gwen had retied her hair, and I could see her seriousness in the set of her chin, more forward than usual, and in the lines around her mouth. She rested an ivory hand on Queen Victoria's shoulder and let herself be led. They stepped in a square a few feet from Louise, who was sitting by herself near the apple juice. Louise smiled encouragement.

I figured the reason Janine hadn't folded with the chair was that she hadn't really been sitting in the first place. Not completely. Not as I sat, with my weight centered in the middle of the seat. She had been holding herself, hovering almost, just above and on the chair, her skin touching metal, but her muscles hard and contracted, on guard against the inevitable, waiting for the dread collapse. Aware of her size, her new (but ultimately old) bigness, her taking up too much space, her being too much in the world. Janine was vigilant toward the possible humiliations her body might bring her, and she was ready when the chair went. More Girl Scout than baton twirler, Janine had been prepared. And always would be.

Do re mi, sang the Jackson Five. Gert went over to Penny and told her to sit out the next song. Penny ran crying from the room.

Me, I never would have picked that chair. I would have sensed its insecurity and chosen another. Syd told me that when I was learning to walk, I didn't fall. Not once. At eighteen months I teetered, arms outstretched, touching sofa, then wall, then ottoman, the tips of my fingers like eyes, taking in everything. Or else I crawled. Between grace and dependence, I found nothing. And hadn't yet.

PART

III

Fifteen

Syd referred to the woman with whom my father had an affair when I was in high school, the woman who ultimately ended their marriage, as the sculptor. She was not a sculptor, not an artist of any kind, not even craftsy, just an unkempt, twenty-three-year-old law student who worked as an intern in my father's office. She wore her wild, bottled-red hair off her face, swept back by a differently patterned strip of cloth each day. The hairstyle showed her large, some might have said unattractive, Roman nose to great effect. When Syd met her at the annual Christmas party, the sculptor was wearing black velvet pants, platform shoes (it was the mid-seventies), and a red velvet vest purchased from a thrift shop. She shook Syd's hand like a man, and Syd noticed that her fingernails were short and exceptionally dirty. Hence the moniker.

Dad told Syd about the affair almost right away. He'd hardly had a choice, his giddy infatuation was so obvious. Syd lived with the infidelity for three months, trying to be modern, then kicked him out after he came home late from the office on a night when they had planned to entertain. Dad had arrived a half hour after the last dinner guest.

Dad and the sculptor lived together for a year in Brookline, and when she left him for a younger man as disheveled as she, Alex went to live with Dad in the two-bedroom garden apartment.

I didn't remember a lot of discussion about Alex's move. There was no custody battle. We all had known it was coming. We had already been divided in our house in Deer Park, the boys against the girls. It was an ongoing competition to determine who was better. When Billie Jean King played Bobby Riggs in the Battle of the Sexes, we four watched it on TV, positioned in couples on separate couches, rooting for our respective genders. We had wagered a fancy dinner that the losing pair would have to cook. Of course, Syd and I won, but the boys got back at us by cooking badly, a fallen soufflé and a too burnt crème brûlée, which, perversely, became proof of their superiority: they couldn't cook and we could. It was the beginning of my understanding of the difference between boys and girls, men and women. Men's failures were often evidence of their virility; women's failures were evidence of its want.

I don't think I ever forgave Alex—we were Irish twins, less than a year apart, and until then, close—for leaving me alone with her.

Dad did not live with anyone after the sculptor. When Alex and I were in college, he went on dates. He even introduced a couple of them to us. But none stayed around for very long. Most of the women had the same unkempt quality as the sculptor; they were not as pretty as our mother.

I remembered, before Dad actually left, the feeling of him wanting to leave her, the feeling of us all wanting to. I remembered the long, silent take-out dinners that Syd and Alex and I ate on the nights Dad had called to say he'd be late, the three of us perched at stand-up wooden trays in front of the tube, Syd insisting on PBS, guilty that we were watching at all. It got so we could watch an owl kill a family of mice—mouse babies included—without losing our appetites.

Alex went to Reed College in Oregon, the beginning of his commitment to the west and to the great outdoors. Summers he worked for Outward Bound. He came home about every other Christmas and talked about physical endurance and euphoria. I went to Boston College and visited

Dad one week, Syd the next. Around the time of my graduation Dad got involved in a study group on masculinity. One
of the partners at work had dragged him to his first meeting,
but since then he'd become a regular, enthusiastic member.
The men read fairy tales and myths that focused on male
power and went on weekend retreats in the woods. They
tested themselves, not physically the way Alex did, but spiri-
tually. They danced and made rituals. They talked about
body hair and authenticity. My fifty-five-year-old father
grew a beard and took up drumming.

During individual, Dana said that children often
make one parent into the good guy, and the other into the
bad guy. She said that my anger at Syd was palpable, but
that my anger for my father had gone completely under-
ground. He was hard to be angry with, it was true. But I
never thought of Syd as the bad guy. She was of the generation of women who sacrificed their own ambitions to have
children. When Alex and I started growing up, and she realized the most important part of parenthood was not imagination but consistency, she also realized that no matter how
interesting we might be, no matter how spectacular our lives
might become, they still wouldn't ever be her life, her ambi-
tion, her desires. How could I be angry at Syd for being
disappointed with that?

I didn't think of Dad as the good guy either. He had
been too interested in being a lawyer and not enough interested in being a dad for me to have strong, happy memories
of him. I remembered the one time he became an active
parent, the year he coached Alex's Little League team. Alex
was a good ball player who could play anywhere in the
infield except the pitcher's mound. Dad made him pitch. The
team lost every game that Alex started. Eventually he quit,
and Dad had to finish out the season without his son.

More than anything else, I was aware of my father's
failures—at tennis, at marriage, at adultery—and I felt sorry
for him. What I didn't feel was respect. Over the years, I
found its absence strenuous.

Sixteen

A my stood in the hall wailing. Mary Beth, Gert, and Amy's individual shrink made a tight circle around her. Penny and Queen Victoria carried Amy's few belongings—junior-miss clothes, stuffed animals, and a huge stack of *Variety*—from her single room to my double. Each time I passed them with my clothes and toiletries, they asked me if I knew what had happened. I shrugged and told them I had no idea. By the third pass, Penny wore a look like, *Right*, and wouldn't meet my eyes. Victoria just smiled, same as anyone's grandmother, wanting to believe the easiest thing.

Usually, the roommate went down to fetch the new arrival, but Amy carried on so, they asked me to escort the new girl onto the floor. I was loath to see Dr. Paul again. Gert said it was the least I could do.

Downstairs, Dr. Paul and Amy's roommate-to-be were chatting at the door to his office. They didn't notice me, so I lingered by the elevators, wanting a private look. A nurse walked past; I knelt to untie, then tie, my shoe.

They talked in near whispers. Still short and self-important, he stood with one arm propped against the door-frame. She was closer to him than I'd ever want to be, arms akimbo, a black clutch bag jutting out like a fan from her hip.

He drew something in the air with his hands. She leaned in to see. All six feet of her. Her tangled, dirty blond hair hovered a foot above Dr. Paul. She wore high-waisted black leather pants and a soft lavender sweater with a giant plunge cut out of the front. As if she were going someplace.

Dr. Paul looked everywhere but at her breasts, the effort visible, his neck twisting as he talked. I walked over. Sweat shone on his forehead. His body was a little, accidental erection. She was the kind of woman I instinctively avoided. I cleared my throat.

"A-hem."

"Oh, yes, Miss . . . um, you've come to collect our recent arrival."

"Forrester," I said, more to her than him. "Alice Forrester."

Her hand was warm and damp, but not unpleasant. She smelled like the outdoors. "Maeve Sullivan."

"Well, I hope you have a pleasant stay," said Dr. Paul.

She smiled at him, holding her head high to avoid the beginning of a double chin. Her features were large, the bones in her face pronounced. Bulimic, I was pretty sure. She squeezed his arm just above the elbow. "I'll be seeing you," she said.

He grinned. "Don't be a stranger."

"Oh, and what about those?" Maeve pointed to a pair of teal blue suitcases, the hard-shelled kind that are made for punishment.

"Leave those to me." He held his hands out at his sides, magnanimous, as if he were offering more than we could see.

"You're too kind," she said.

"It's true." He nodded.

He seemed to not know he was being flattered. It made me uncomfortable.

"I'm too kind."

Seventeen

Maeve asked to tour the first floor before going upstairs.

I said, "But they have things planned."

She walked past me into the lecture hall, her outdoor smell trailing. It was like the ground after rain. At first I thought it was simply the smell of someone living outside of Seaview. But it was richer. Oily. I skipped a step to catch up.

I said, "It's not that I care personally. It's just, I think you have your first session with your individual shrink today."

She fingered the corny posters and plaques. "I'm in no rush."

I followed her to the cafeteria. We surveyed the crowd but didn't go in. The fourth-floor addicts were enjoying a sullen lunch, their heads bent over their trays with deliberation. I explained that we didn't eat together because they could eat whatever they wanted.

Maeve did not seem anxious or surprised by anything. I pointed out the gym facilities at the end of the hall. She nodded at the four adjacent rooms.

"You ever swim in the pool?" she asked, as we turned around.

I shook my head.

"Why not?"

"It's dinky. You can't do laps."

"Who would want to?"

"Well, just about everyone here, I think."

"Not me."

"You don't swim?"

"I think of exercise as a form of corporal punishment." She laughed, and her sweater slipped off one shoulder, exposing a black bra strap and a fleshy upper arm.

It was a prepared joke, something she had said before.

"But it's good for you, exercise."

She didn't respond.

Her skin was spotted with freckles dark as moles. I followed their trail down her throat, across the collarbones, toward the slit between her breasts. Maybe some of them actually were moles. She hiked the fallen sleeve into place.

Heading back toward the stairs, we stopped at the lecture hall again.

"Could you hold this a second?"

Her clutch bag.

The room was quiet and empty, but I could still feel the reverberations of the weekly mixed meeting.

"We're already late," I said. "They'll be looking for us."

Underneath the large placard announcing the Twelve Steps was a small wastepaper basket. She picked it up. A clingy clear plastic bag lined the inside. She held the wastebasket under her chin with one hand and jammed the other into her mouth. Her eyes got wide, and her big, man's jaw jutted forward. There was almost a click when her fingers found the gag spot, like the bones in her neck connecting, but she made no guttural sound.

I stepped out of the room.

I had pictured them doing it with one, maybe two fingers. But she had a wide, rubbery mouth, and was able to cram in all her fingers plus the fat thumb, right up to the second knuckle, just short of a fist.

I looked up and down the hall. I said, "That was pretty stupid. Anyone could have walked by."

"I couldn't help it," she said. "Paul—Dr. Sampson said I could call him Paul—he gave me some kinda tranquilizer." She put down the basket. "I hate tranquilizers."

"He says everyone can call him Paul, and you should lower your voice." I stepped back in the room. It smelled of sour milk and turnips; the rain was gone. I wanted to get out of there.

"A hundred milligrams of anything," she said, "and I feel like I'm moving through Jell-O." She reached into her front pants pocket with her clean hand and retrieved a small white square. "That was one thing I could never understand in high school—kids who did downs. Ups always made sense to me, but downs? I'm already down, you know what I mean? Why else would I be doing pills?" She put a corner of the plastic package in her mouth and tore along a precut line. Inside was a familiar antiseptic towelette.

I hadn't known anyone in high school who'd done ups or downs. I said, "So you really plan for this?"

She laughed, then wiped her fist and the corners of her mouth. She had big teeth. "Don't you?" She threw the dirty towelette in the wastebasket.

I felt suddenly self-conscious, as if I'd been doing things halfway. I said, "How come you use your whole hand?"

"It works better. Everything comes up." She took her purse, which I'd been holding all this time. "It's not like when you puke regularly, from being sick. That starts lower down and brings up more. I used to have to do it two or three times to get everything out of there, depending on the meal. I mean, you can just forget about spaghetti, for instance." She found a pot of lip gloss in her bag and unscrewed the cap.

"And why not, you know, in the toilet?"

She held the glistening container out to me.

I shook my head.

She dipped her middle finger and traced a greasy sheen on her cracked lips. "I got tired of putting my face where other people shit," she said. "It was giving me low self-esteem."

At last. Someone with a sense of humor.

Eighteen

The next day, Maeve slept through meditation. At breakfast, Amy said she had tried to wake Maeve several times, speaking softly at first and finally grabbing her bare shoulder and shaking. Amy said that Maeve had told her to fuck off.

At ten-thirty, Gert escorted Maeve to group therapy. Maeve took the chair next to mine, smiling as if she were thrilled to see me. She grabbed my arm above the elbow and squeezed, her thumb in the crease. People stared. She was really something: the least ravaged-looking bulimic on the floor. No broken capillaries or purple circles. Her teeth were a model's set, square and straight and perfectly white. The only indication was her lips, chapped and split like the others'.

Amy refused to look at Maeve. She crossed her arms and legs and dropped her head. The leg that crossed wrapped twice around the stationary one.

I watched the girls discover Maeve: the same leather pants, this time with a ribbed mustard sweater, another clutch bag. She placed it under her chair. We'd all assumed carrying purses was illegal here; no one else did. The pants made a soft sucking sound when she sat down beside me. She had a big behind, bigger even than Janine's. It entirely covered the seat of her chair.

Gert rested her hands on the tops of her thighs. We could see the outline of her legs beneath the folds of her dress. I didn't understand why all the couselors at Seaview weren't thin. It annoyed me. Gert asked Maeve to share something about herself that nobody knew.

"Lemme think." Maeve pulled all ten fingers through her hair. "Absolutely nobody?" She brought her fist to her mouth and gnawed the knuckle of her tucked-in thumb. "I don't think there's anything *nobody* knows."

Gert smiled. "Something private then."

"Lemme think." She thought for a long time. We fidgeted. None of us tolerated silence well. Gert was just about to say something when Maeve said, "Okay. I know. Not too many people know this. How about, I fart when I come."

Gert sighed.

"Not every time," said Maeve.

The rest of us made choking laughs.

I wondered whether Gert minded this—hostile resistance, according to Dana—or was she just so used to it?

Gert smiled again at Maeve. Her ears and neck were flushed. She was working to keep the anger or embarrassment, whatever it was, from her face. "We might as well get started. You'll learn more about the group from seeing us in action anyway. And vice versa. This morning, I'd like to talk about our jobs. Let's hear what everyone does for a living, whether or not you like it, and what you might like to do instead."

Just then the door to the group room swung open. "I'm sorry I'm late." It was Louise.

Maeve was across the room before I'd noticed she'd left her chair. "Louise!" she shouted. "Louise! Louise!" She talked and touched at once. First Louise's hair, then her Big Men's jeans, then the thick, blunt wrists. They had been in the same rehab in Florida. Cellmates, Maeve announced, clapping Louise's hands together. Louise took a half step back. Then another. I'd never seen anyone touch her.

Gert played the killjoy, getting them to sit. Maeve found a chair for Louise and opened it next to her own, forcing a space on her left. I was glad she hadn't moved me.

Gert made us return to "What's Your Line," starting with the suddenly popular Louise.

Louise took a moment to catch her breath. The excitement had flooded her heart. She gulped air and bit her lip. She smiled at Maeve. "I've always wanted to write, instead of proofread, science fiction."

Terrific, I thought, I can't wait to read about the planet of the morbidly obese.

We went around the circle.

Penny said, "I really have to find something other than the aerobics. Something outside of fitness altogether. It's good money." She looked crestfallen, but she was learning what to say. "But it just feeds my disease."

There was nodding all around the room.

"I think I'm going to retire when I get back," said Queen Victoria. "I've been a nutritionist for the last nine years. It's the only thing I know how to do. I'm afraid of too much free time, though. Idle hands," she said gravely.

More nodding.

Gwen was next. She said she didn't work. She volunteered at museums and hospitals. She read out loud once a week to an elderly blind woman. She studied the oboe. We had a hard time following; her sentences trailed off, unfinished.

"Does that mean you're financially independent?" Gert asked.

Gwen brought her shoulders to her ears, then nodded. It was an apology.

Maeve snorted.

Little Amy talked about a commercial she starred in several years ago. "First I'm in the front seat. Then the back. Then I'm just sitting in the tire."

No one could remember it.

"What kind of car was it?" asked Penny.

"A station wagon," said Amy. "But the ad was for the tire, not the car."

People grumbled.

"What are you wearing?" asked Gert.

Amy cleared her throat, opened a new lozenge. "Just a diaper."

Gert looked exasperated. "Well, no wonder we didn't recognize you. Is there anything more recent? Something where you look more like yourself, today?"

Amy shook her head. More grumbling. More speculation about her acting career. Amy stuck her fingers in her ears and started humming.

Gert said, "Amy, quit it."

She stopped humming but did not drop her hands.

Gert said, "Let's move along."

I explained my job as an archivist at Boston College, where I had received my undergraduate degree in history and was still working on my masters.

"No kidding." Maeve grabbed my arm. I got a whiff of yesterday's perfume. She said, "I'm a librarian."

"Where?"

"Quincy Junior College, special collections."

She didn't look like a librarian. She moved too much. Most of the librarians I knew were capable of stillness.

Louise said, "New job?"

Maeve turned in her chair, the leather pants crinkling.

Louise said, "You weren't in special collections before."

"No, you're right." Maeve grabbed Louise's thigh. It shook. "I've left microfiche for good." She sat back. "Boy, it's nice to have someone who knows you in a place like this."

Gert said, "Do any of you feel that your eating disorder has in some way hampered your careers? Has kept you from your heart's desires?"

Just when you forgot she was in the room.

Maeve rolled her eyes. We all were quiet except Louise; we could hear her breathing. After group therapy, there was a free period.

Maeve said, "How about you?"

We looked at Gert.

Maeve said, "What about your heart's desire?"

Gert said, "I'd rather hear about yours."

"I bet you would."

More silence.

"This can't be it," asked Maeve, "can it? Being here with us?"

Gert hesitated.

"I hope not, for your sake," said Maeve.

"Why do you say that?" Gert folded her hands in her lap.

"So you have an eating disorder, so you get better, and you spend the rest of your life talking to other people about their eating disorders? That's it? That's your life?"

"I don't exactly look at it that way."

Maeve said, "How do you look at it, then? I'd be interested to know."

Gert started to speak, then stopped. It had begun innocently enough. We asked her questions about her life all the time, and she usually managed to provide a perfect recovering example. She said, "This work keeps my head out of the toilet. Period." She grasped her knees with her hands and rocked forward. "That is my heart's desire. To not spend every day of my g.d. life on the floor of the g.d. bathroom. To not have memorized the whereabouts of every public toilet in the city of Boston. To not know which fancy restaurants and theaters have bathroom attendants. To not have black-and-blues on the caps of my knees."

Maeve looked deliberately bored.

"Now, shall we?" said Gert. "I'd like to learn about someone else's heart's desire."

But it was too late. The thought was in the room: all we could ever hope for was this. Hospitals and fifty-minute hours and group process. Church basements with folding metal chairs. Not to do the strange things we did with food.

That was it. We could never have what we really wanted, which was simply more. More than what we'd gotten. More than somebody else.

I looked at Maeve. She was staring at a spot on the wall behind Gert. I leaned over. "I like that perfume you wear."

She turned to me and smiled. It took her eyes a minute to focus. *"Pluie,"* she said. "It's French."

Nineteen

―――――

After group therapy, Maeve and I went to the rec room. We had twenty minutes before lunch. It was empty when we arrived and Maeve turned on the TV first thing. The rec room was identical to the group room, only at the opposite end of the unit. It had sofas and a Ping-Pong table instead of folding mats and chairs. Maeve opened her clutch bag and took out a pack of cigarettes. "Smoke?" she said.

"It's illegal," I said.

"I didn't ask if it was legal," said Maeve. "I asked if you wanted one."

"It's the matches, really, that are illegal, not the cigarettes themselves."

"Smoke?" she said again.

I cleared my throat. "Sure, why not." I never had.

She handed me the cigarettes still in their cellophane packaging. "Do you mind?"

While I fumbled with the wrapper, she raised the purse to her chin and puked into it. Not much came up. She repeated her towelette ritual from the day before, finding the little plastic square in her pants pocket and depositing it, used, into the purse, which she snapped shut. It smelled like spoiled fruit.

"God, I hate corn flakes," she said. "You'd think they'd serve something with a little more flavor. Are you all right?"

I must have lost some color. "Your bag," I said through clenched teeth, trying to hold my breath.

She grinned. "There's more where that came from. I have quite an assortment. What happened to that smoke, then?" She put the defiled clutch on top of the TV and took the cigarette pack out of my hands. I thought, She's showing off for me. She withdrew two cigarettes and gave me one.

I held it between my lips, as I figured I should, down-turned and slightly to one side. She lit hers first. I bet she smoked to cover the smell of her vomiting. It almost worked. The flame of the match was at her fingertips when I realized she was holding it out for me. By the time I leaned forward, she had extinguished the flame.

"Shit," she said. "Just learning how at your age?" She took my cigarette, put it in her mouth, and touched it with the end of hers. The red tips glistened. She handed mine back, then took a drag of her own. She pointed at the big green table. "Ping-Pong?"

"I don't play."

"Chickenshit." She tilted her head back to exhale.

"It's a stupid game."

"If not Ping-Pong, what then?"

"Huh?"

"Are you going to take a drag of that?"

I looked down at my cigarette. There was a red lipstick stain on one end and already too much ash at the other. I wondered if it would taste like corn flakes. Maeve held out her palm, cupped into an ashtray. I flicked.

She said, "What is there to do here for fun?"

I brought the cigarette to my lips, sniffing surreptitiously before puffing. There was nothing. I put it in my mouth and drew a breath. It felt like thick steam, only scratchy. I blew it out. "There is no fun here," I said.

"I find that hard to believe."

"It's true. Ask anyone. Ask your best friend, Louise."

She took a very deep drag on her cigarette and put it out against the bottom of her high-heeled shoe. She held the butt in her ashtray-palm. "Who said Louise was my best friend?"

I took another cigarette breath. She made me nervous.

She said, "This your first time in rehab?"

I nodded.

"Thought so."

"You?"

"Numero five."

"No kidding."

"I've been all over."

I couldn't imagine. "Why did you . . . I mean, it can't be that they're going to tell you anything new?"

"One more." She pointed to my cigarette. I inhaled deeper and the smoke slid down the back of my throat. I started coughing. I coughed for a while. She took the cigarette and pounded my back until I was bent in half.

When I could speak, I said, "Were the other rehabs like this?"

"More or less." She was smoking the rest of mine.

"How come you came here?"

"The food."

I laughed out loud and started hacking again. This time she didn't pound my back, though I was still hunched over.

She waited until I stopped coughing, then said, "How come you came here?"

"I had no choice. They brought me in an ambulance."

She extinguished my cigarette the same way she did hers, then bent over and put her face next to mine, questioning.

"I had a heart attack. I was at Medical first, then they transferred me."

"How much did you weigh?"

We straightened up.

"I got under ninety."

She whistled and took a step back. She looked down the length of my body. "How tall are you?"

Then we did some math together. It was the same math I did my first morning at Psychiatric, and the same math I did, with variations, every day after. I told her my height, five ten and three-quarters, my current weight, and how the insurance charts and *Vogue* allowed between three and five pounds for every inch after five feet. I told her that although Gwen weighed less in real pounds—I estimated eighty-five or eighty-six, with eighty-three as the absolute low—she was only five feet six, which meant she weighed at least five pounds more than me.

Maeve said, "So I guess you can never be too rich or too thin, huh?"

"Something like that." I watched her face. I couldn't tell what she thought. She was maybe fifteen pounds past the high end of the insurance chart for her height.

"Another cigarette?" she asked.

I shook my head.

She pulled one from the pack.

Louise and Gwen came in. The three of us watched Maeve smoke her third cigarette. Louise agreed to Ping-Pong. Gwen and I sat in chairs alongside the table and called out the score.

Twenty

———

A t breakfast, Maeve and Louise were seated at our table. Louise and Gwen and I usually ate together. Not out of any great love; Louise and I still shared food whenever we could.

Louise was in her regular spot, a blue velvet love seat large enough for two, and Maeve sat next to her in Gwen's chair, a straight-backed walnut with brocaded cushions. I got my bowl of cereal from the serving window and brought it to the table. Neither of them looked up. Gwen arrived after me, cereal bowl between pallid hands, her eyes watching the swim of the milk as it lapped the bowl's edge. She took the last seat, a chrome and vinyl kitchen chair, and mouthed *good morning*.

"Nice meditation," I said too loud, wanting to get Maeve's attention.

"Mm."

"Gert did a lovely job, considering."

Considering?

I leaned forward. The difference between Gwen's voiced and mimicked words was so slight, I could never be sure whether she had actually spoken. I said, "Considering Mary Beth's absence."

"Mm."

They persisted in their private conversation. Maeve was twisted in her chair, facing Louise, all four of her long limbs crossed, her elbow on the velvet arm of Louise's love seat. Their friendship didn't make sense to me.

I said to Gwen, "I particularly like the Salutation to the Sun."

"*Which one is that?*" She used her whole face to ask, as if she had a daily limit to the number of words she could speak.

"The one that starts with your hands together, like a prayer."

"Mm."

I heard Louise say something about astronomy. Her intimacy with Maeve was infuriating. I mashed my blue corn flakes against the sides and bottom of my bowl. Gwen sat still with her hands in her lap. I had never seen her eat. I knew she did; her plate emptied at every meal. But without any visible effort from her, as though she thought the appearance of appetite was worse than the fact of it. I bet I could catch her in flagrante delicto. I said, "Have you ever tried the blue corn flakes?"

She shook her head.

"Taste?" I offered the bowl. Even though I did not eat my cereal, I insisted on blue rather than yellow corn flakes.

"*No, thank you.*" She looked embarrassed.

It would not be as easy as that. I said, "Expecting any visitors this week?"

She nodded.

"Parents?"

"My fiancé."

"I didn't realize you had a fiancé."

Maeve's head turned. "Who has a fiancé?"

I pointed at Gwen, who was unfolding a paper napkin in her lap.

Maeve recrossed her legs and aimed her body toward us. "I didn't know people still got engaged." She bounced the top leg against the bottom one. She was wearing a coffee-colored suede miniskirt, red silk blouse, and black stockings. I was never a woman like this.

"When are you doing it?" asked Maeve.

"You never mentioned a fiancé," said Louise.

"We haven't set the date," said Gwen.

"Let's see the rock."

Gwen dug into the front pocket of her jeans and pulled out the ring. She slipped it on her finger. Maeve reached across the table and grabbed Gwen's hand. Gwen came half out of her chair, following her own wrist and fingers. I could see the flesh-colored Band-Aid that was supposed to keep the ring in place.

Maeve said, "How long have you been engaged?"

Gwen came free and eased down into her chair. She counted the years on her fingers, bending them back and exposing the bones in each palm. The ring slipped on her finger until the diamond pointed down. Finally she held up both hands, fingers splayed.

"Ten years?"

Gwen nodded.

Maeve said, "Why buy the cow when you get the milk for free, huh?"

Gwen flushed. "No. It's not that. It's just. Hank."

"Hank?" asked Maeve. "That's his name?"

Gwen nodded. *Hank.* Isn't. Sure."

"Not sure?" Maeve looked at Louise and me. "Ten years, and he's not sure. What can he possibly not be sure about?"

"Hank wants babies."

"And you don't?"

Gwen waved away the thought. "I love children. And want to have them." She took off the ring and put it back in her pocket. "It's just."

"It's just what?"

"I haven't. You know, *ovulated.* In seven years."

Maeve whistled.

"Hank says he doesn't mind. Waiting. He wants to be sure I'm better. Before."

"Sounds like a real prince," said Maeve.

"He's very patient, Hank."

I could tell Gwen meant it.

Louise said, "You never mentioned any of this."

"You never asked." Gwen felt along the back of her head for the tightness of her French braid, which was perfectly intact. When she took her hand away, several wisps came undone.

Maeve said, "Do you guys still do it?"

Gwen cleared her throat and picked up her spoon. She rummaged in her bowl of yellow flakes.

"I didn't think so," said Maeve. "See, that's the thing about long-term relationships. No sex. I don't know anybody who's managed to keep fucking past the three-year mark. Do you?"

Gwen brought a soggy pile to her mouth and slid the spoon between her lips. I watched her delicate, Mayflower jaw. She did not chew. Strands of her flat white hair loosened themselves.

"Personally," said Maeve, "I've never made it past six months without the sex taking a nosedive."

I looked around the table. Maeve probably had had more sex than the three of us combined.

"What's the best sex you've ever had?" she said. "Come on. Everyone has to tell."

Gwen swallowed her corn flakes, the muscles on her long neck constricting, one after another. Louise pretended to be busy in her bowl of cold oatmeal; it was almost empty; she scraped the sides. I thought about my one sexual encounter with Ronald. How could I make it sound more elaborate than it'd been?

"Okay, chickenshits," said Maeve. "I'll go first. Best ever was this poet who was having a midlife crisis. Said he'd suddenly gotten conscious of his own mortality. His dick never went down. I mean it did, but it didn't. Not hardly." She laughed at her accidental pun. No one else did.

"We did it in a coffeehouse where he was reading. During intermission. In the coat room."

The cafeteria got very quiet. I could feel the others listening.

Maeve said, "Okay, who's next? Alice? You go."

I didn't want everyone to hear. I spoke softly. "Nothing out of the ordinary," I said.

"What?" said Maeve. "Speak up, for Christ's sake. I can't hear you."

"Just the regular. I've only done the regular thing." I didn't say *once*.

Maeve made the sound of a buzzer going off. "Next. Gwen?"

Gwen concentrated on her cereal bowl and did not lift her head.

"It's all up to you, Louise." Maeve punched her arm. "Don't let us down."

I thought, This will be a quick game. Just the idea of Louise that way made me queasy. But all of a sudden, Louise let out a breathy giggle, and said, "Boston Edison."

Maeve said, "What are we talking about here? Customer services?"

Louise nodded.

"Be specific."

I remembered they knew each other from before. Perhaps Louise had already played this game. She said, "The meter-reading guys." There was foam at one corner of her mouth.

Gwen looked up. I made a small noise, involuntarily, at the back of my throat. I swear I hadn't meant to.

Louise glared at me. "Some men like fat, you know. I don't know why, but it's true. Some men would pick me over you."

I closed my eyes.

"So what happened?" Maeve sounded anxious. "You met them at the door in Saran Wrap?"

"More or less," said Louise.

Maeve said, "It's the more or less that we came for, Louise. I said be specific. You know the rules."

I opened my eyes. Louise was glancing over her shoulder. She whispered, "Let's just say Boston Edison believes in customer satisfaction."

"Louise!" Maeve shouted. She slammed the table with her fist. Our dishes jumped. "You're not playing fair."

I looked around. The whole room was watching now. Gert came over.

"Morning, ladies," she said. "Everyone enjoying her meal?"

No one spoke.

She took a step toward Maeve. "Getting used to us?"

Everyone knew the two of them hadn't hit it off. Maeve stared at her fist in the middle of the table.

I smiled at Gert. "We were just debating the merits of 'Acting as If' versus 'Having Your True Feelings.' I'm never sure when to do which."

Gert circled us, her hands behind her back. Her dress had purple and yellow roses on it, each flower as big as an outstretched hand. A wallpaper dress. "It's more or less both." She looked quickly from face to face, trying to intercept a facetious look. "Always 'Have Your True Feelings' first. 'Act as If' to get through the day."

Gwen and Louise and I nodded.

Gert put a hand on my shoulder. "Nice to see you thinking about your recovery."

She knew I was lying. I said, "I guess it was bound to sink in after a while."

"Bound to." Gert's hand slid partway down my back, grazing the top few vertebrae, which stuck out, I had been told, like the rungs of a ladder. She pulled her hand away quickly.

I turned around. "Osmosis."

"It does work something like that," she said. She

rubbed her hands together, then hid them in the pockets of her wallpaper dress. She circled the table again. She eyed Maeve. "See you all later."

We took a breath. I permitted myself a genuine smile.

Nice job, mouthed Gwen. Louise nodded.

Maeve unclenched her fist and flexed her fingers. "What about public places?" she said.

"What?"

She turned to me. Her eyes were bright and black, the cloudy green irises eclipsed by spreading pupils. "Where's the most public place you've ever had sex?"

I felt funny. She wouldn't stop.

Gwen got up and carried her bowl and spoon to the serving window. Her bowl was empty, and I'd seen her swallow only once.

"Come on," said Maeve.

I shook my head.

Gwen sat back down. Her hair continued to unfasten.

"Louise?" Maeve asked.

"Nothing public," said Louise.

Maeve said, "On a 727 en route to Kalamazoo. With the pilot."

"In the cockpit?" I asked.

"No, in first class. The plane was practically empty."

"And who was—"

"The copilot flew the plane," she said.

It occurred to me that she was lying. I said, "And the stewardess? Where was she during all this?"

"The stewardess watched," said Maeve. "Okay, let's try something easier. Everyone can play. The first time you fell in love."

I didn't like this game. "What were you doing in Kalamazoo?"

"I mean the real thing," said Maeve. "Stupid in love."

"Hank," said Gwen.

"Of course," said Maeve. "Handsome Hank. How did you fall in love?"

Gwen blinked and pulled at her renegade hair. The fallen strands drooped around her face like an elderly lion's mane.

"What made you love him?" asked Maeve.

"Oh, the oboe," she said.

"The oboe?"

"He plays with the Boston Pops. *First oboe.*" She held up one finger, proud of Hank.

"He plays good?"

"Very." Gwen smiled. "But it's more than that. It's how he treats the oboe."

"How-he-treats-the-oboe?" said Maeve.

Gwen nodded. She was a little slow-moving for Maeve.

"So how does he treat the goddamn oboe?" Maeve hissed.

"Like a sacred object," said Gwen.

I'd never heard her say so much at once.

"And that appealed to you?" asked Maeve.

Gwen nodded. "Mother always said Father treated her like a sacred object. That's how I knew."

"Knew what?"

"Hank was the one."

Maeve turned to Louise. "I didn't think people still talked like this."

Louise wore a look that said, It's news to me.

Maeve scratched behind her ear. "Your turn," she said to me.

I shrugged. "I've never been in love."

"Liar," she said with a laugh.

"What's that supposed to mean?"

She laughed again.

I truly hated this game.

"I guess it's up to me," said Maeve.

Which was when I realized she'd been waiting all this time for the chance to tell. Our stories hadn't mattered.

Maeve said, "I was in love once with a fifteen-year-old French boy named Valentin. I was twenty-one, and working as his little sister's au pair in Paris."

I had read about people like Maeve. She was compelled to show us private things. Like those men in raincoats, only she did it with words. Our whole conversation had been preparation for this.

She said, "He taught me French while I chased fucking little Marie-Alix back and forth from school. When she finally passed out after a full day of terrorizing me, he and I would read out loud together."

"That's pretty," said Gwen, *"Marie-Alix."*

"Yeah, well there was nothing pretty about that kid," said Maeve. "Lemme tell you, she was a dominatrix at seven."

Gwen covered a smile. Louise made her frothy giggle.

I could picture the two of them, Maeve and Marie-Alix. The little girl's hair was probably never clean. She had wide-set eyes and an expression that her parents would worry about when she was older. Maeve was thinner then.

She said, "I sat on the floor with the book in my lap, my back against his bed frame, and Valentin lay stretched out across the bed, reading over my shoulder." I saw her long, dungareed legs on the parquet floor—he had asked his parents for the exact same jeans—her thick hair bunched around her shoulders, half on the wrinkled white sheets, half off.

"He corrected my pronunciation as I read the sex parts from *Madame Bovary,* only there aren't any sex parts in the whole fucking book. Just long descriptions of the garden and how she tips her head back to get every drop of sherry from the glass and everyone's tits heaving all the time."

"I love that scene in the inn," said Louise, "when she meets her first lover, Léon, I think."

Maeve frowned at Louise.

Louise shrugged. "It's one of my favorite books."

"And then what happened?" I wanted the rest.

Maeve said, "He was fucking exquisite. Pubescent but not quite through it."

I pictured Maeve's red American mouth trying to make the French *u* sound; the boy leaning over from behind, his shoulder tipped against hers, the bones pinching. He pointed to the word, not *oo*, he repeated the sound, *u*, as in *"tu es mignonne."* Maeve would not have been able to hear the difference.

She said, "He was boy and girl at once. Eyes without any sadness yet. I climbed on top of him. He was warm all over, like he'd just popped out of the oven. He came twice before he even got inside me."

She must have weighed more than him, even relatively thin as she was then. And what did he think, the fifteen-year-old whose mother and grandmother and two aunts (one was divorced and living right next door) were thin like canes? Did he think, *This is too much* or *just enough* or *I want more?* She would have been a lot. For anyone.

"We did it practically every night after, with his parents in the next room."

Perhaps she had lied before. About the middle-aged poet. About the pilot. But this story, I was sure, this boy and his sister, all of it was true. The green was coming back into her eyes. Her pupils tunneled in on themselves.

Twenty-one

In art therapy, Maeve refused to do anything. Cass offered to trace her outline, but Maeve said she preferred to watch and think. Cass let Maeve plan her drawing for a few days. "You'll have to at least make an attempt by Friday," said Cass. She treated us like this was truly art, like we were artists. She said she believed in our creative processes.

Gwen worked almost exclusively on the hair. She used skinny scraps of construction paper and feathers. First she collected all the yellow and orange feathers, not a true representation of her particular blond, which was just short of albino. And she made it long and fluffy on the drawing, with a sixties flip, instead of bound up the way she actually wore it. In the body drawing her hair had texture and high-lights—the construction paper was all different colors and showed through the canary-colored feathers—whereas in life her hair was so flat and thin that at times it looked painted on. Once, at the pool, I had thought it was a bathing cap, pin-straight, flowerless, and plastered to her skull.

Gwen layered feathers over construction paper over feathers over construction paper, until the head grew larger than the body. Then she worked on the shoes, duct-tape patent leathers. The drawing was distorted. A big-headed, big-footed child. She was quite pleased.

Louise did not sit on the floor to do her drawing. She needed the hard, structured support of a chair to sit comfort-ably, though once she was seated, she was unable to reach the outline. Cass suggested that Louise tape it to the wall and work standing up. Louise colored in half of her body drawing this way. She used a black crayon and scribbled quickly. By midway through the class, the outline was jet black from her toes to her belly. Maeve had gone over to Louise's drawing. The two of them stood examining the half-black, life-size diamond.

Cass looked dismayed. "Louise, dear," she said, "the internal landscape is a bit bleak, a bit one-dimensional."

Louise took a step back from the drawing.

"Do you follow me when I say 'internal landscape'?" asked Cass. "Are you with me, dear?"

My own drawing was barely begun, but the outline did resemble me. I ran my finger along the edge, which blurred from my retracing it. It was an odd-looking triangle, much more narrow at the top than at the bottom, where my legs had opened for the jumping jack. I sat down next to it and tried to decide once and for all whether I was an ectomorph or mesomorph.

Cass noticed my inactivity. She came and stood silently by my empty drawing, chin in hand, the tips of her fingers brushing the line of her mouth. I picked up a blue pencil and began coloring along the edge of the outline. I decided, for no reason other than she might ask, that my internal landscape would be clouds.

Twenty-two

___

Maeve was at my door. She said, "So how'd you manage this?"

"Manage what?"

"This single room."

"Oh, this."

She smiled and pulled her hair off her face. I had just come from doing laundry and was sitting on my bed, matching socks.

She said, "I mean, who'd you have to sleep with?"

I said, "My mother got the room."

She waited as if she knew there were more.

"Plus I stole some of the girls' clothes after exercise class, and they happen to think I'm a pervert."

This seemed to please her. She stepped in and closed the door.

My new room was a replica of the last, only a third less wide. Pencil-shaped with a high, square window that didn't open out or in. It threw a patch of waning light on the mirror that hung against my door. Maeve looked at her reflection, fixed her hair. The light made it difficult for her to see her full image. She stood a foot back from the mirror and shielded her eyes. I stopped matching socks and waited.

Maeve said, "What's she like, your mother?"

"It's hard to say."

"If you only had one word."

I thought a minute. "Relentless."

"Big word," she said.

"Not too big for Syd."

"Syd? She sounds like a little old man, like she walks stooped over."

"Well, she doesn't. She's quite beautiful."

"When's her next visit?"

"They won't let her."

The light glared against the mirror in such a way that Maeve appeared to have no middle. She put her hands on her hips. She twisted from side to side. "What's she do?"

"Nothing for a long time. Now she's a matrimonial consultant."

"A what?"

I got off my bed and went to my chest of drawers. I knew I had a picture. "She helps you pick your bridesmaids' dress, the menu, the band. All that."

"She must like weddings."

"That's an understatement. She spends at least two days a week in bridal boutiques, just getting ideas." I found it: the four of us at Old Silver Beach, a year or two before the divorce.

Maeve said, "What kind of ideas?"

"Oh, you know. Traditional Southern versus French Country. Her favorite wedding is a snowball wedding. All the women wear white. They usually have those in December. We were in a bridal shop when I had the heart attack."

I brought her the picture. She bent over it, still facing the mirror. The sun was going down. I should have turned on the light but didn't. She said, "Nice-looking woman. Nice-looking family. When was this taken? You weighed more then."

"I was in high school."

"You look just like your brother."

"People say that, but I don't see it."

"All that black hair. Is he still handsome?"

"I guess."

"And is he allowed to visit?"

"He's allowed, but he won't. He's in Alaska. He works for one of those outfits that teach businessmen wilderness skills. They're supposed to get scared into cooperating with each other. Trust by default. Half the time we can't even reach him. Which is how he likes it. Syd wrote him to tell him I'm here, but she hasn't heard back."

"Come here," she said. "I want to show you something." She pulled me in front of her. "Look at yourself there." She pointed at our reflection. She was half in the mirror, one tightly blue-jeaned thigh, one frilly white arm; I was completely captured. I hated my clothes. L. L. Bean and Land's End.

"Now look at this." She showed me the photo again.

I remembered the bathing suit. Syd and I had fought over it. There were boats, anchors, seashells, a nautical motif. She had thought it looked childish.

Maeve said, "Not for nothing, but you look about a thousand times better with a few pounds on you."

"Gee, no one's ever said that before."

She held the picture up, and we looked at its reflection in the mirror. "I mean at least here you've got some tits."

"Not for nothing," I said, "you could lose a few pounds yourself."

She said, "Fuck you," and handed me the picture.

The sun had practically disappeared. The light in my room was flat. We were quiet. I didn't want to apologize, but I didn't want her to leave. After a while Maeve said, "What were you doing when you had the heart attack?"

"Oh, shopping. Trying on dresses."

"Bridesmaids' dresses?"

"No, wedding gowns. I was wearing one when I collapsed. The EMTs had to cut me out of it."

"Don't most brides pick their own dresses?"

"They do. Syd just likes them. Likes seeing me in them."

"Sounds pretty fucking weird."

I shrugged. "It's what we do together. Don't you do certain things with certain people—rituals, like?"

"Oh yes," she said, and, as if in answer to my question, she began unbuttoning her blouse.

I had a sudden flash of the young French boy and his sister whom Maeve had taken care of. She had said that the parents were in the next room when she and Valentin had sex, that they had never found out. For the first time I wondered about little Marie-Alix, who was supposed to have been sleeping. I wondered whether she had ever wandered in. Maeve unsnapped her bra in the back and pulled the straps down, under her sleeves. The bra dropped. It was beige lace but ratty. She pulled the blouse off her shoulders and wore it like a stole.

I didn't know what to say. I tried to look her in the eye.

She said, "I could never be anorexic."

"Oh?" I felt panicky.

"I couldn't give these up."

I had to look. They were big—I couldn't remember having seen any bigger—easily a D. The areolas covered half of them and looked like little plum-colored French berets. She pressed the heel of her palms into the nipples.

I heard voices in the hall. Louise and Gwen. Coming closer. Maeve started to laugh. I would get kicked out for this. I covered Maeve's mouth. Gwen knocked and called my name. They waited. All they had to do was open the door—there were no locks on patient rooms. My elbow pressed against one of Maeve's buoyant breasts. I was afraid she thought I was enjoying this. At last they walked away. Maeve's chin was pink where my hand had been. I took a step toward the foot of the bed.

Maeve turned back to the mirror and took out her little pot of lip gloss. She touched up her lips. "I don't know how you stand it," she said.

"Stand what?"

"Don't you miss them?"

I shrugged. I could feel the heat on my skin. I thought of the words I knew for breasts that implied Maeve's size: *hooters, knockers, jugs.* I said, "I'm not sure I ever really had them."

"But you had more than this." Maeve pulled me in front of the mirror again. She pointed at the reflection.

"I guess so."

"I bet you did. I bet you had those pert little breasts that the athletic girls had. Breasts that played field hockey and lacrosse."

I could not hold still.

"Your turn," she said.

"What?"

"Show and tell."

I think I probably went from red to white.

"Come on," she breathed. "Louise does."

I stood still while she undid my shirt, then pulled my turtleneck over my head. I didn't know what disturbed me more: the possibility that it was true, that she looked at Louise like this, or that she had made it up just to persuade me. With my two tops off, I could smell myself.

"That's the show part," she said, facing the mirror again. "Now tell. Tell me something I don't already know."

I had always liked my anorexic reflection. It meant seeing the parts instead of the whole. Each connection, each articulation of muscle, skin, and bone made explicit. Gert said that we all had distorted images of ourselves. Either fatter or skinnier than we really were. She said we hated our bodies, hated ourselves. I had never thought so. But it was shocking to see me in the mirror next to Maeve, my flesh concave wherever hers stuck out. We looked unreal. Everything of hers—teeth, nose, eyes—was bigger. She had moles the size of dimes. I seemed unfinished next to her. Folds of skin drooped below my nipples. The words people used to describe my breasts were food words: *pancakes* and *two fried eggs* and *sunny-side up*. Breakfast words. I said, "You like being"—I wasn't sure how to say it—"admired."

She said, "Yes."

She said, "Don't you?"

I shook my head.

"I thought everyone did." Maeve bent to pick up her bra. Her breasts hung in great points, like funnels; they jiggled against her stomach. She straightened and slipped off her blouse, one arm at a time. She put on the bra. It had a wire, like my mother's. She had to fit the lace part around each breast. I said, "Doesn't that hurt?"

"What?"

"The wire thingie."

"The underwire?"

"Yes."

"It hurts if I don't wear it. They get tired."

I said, "Breasts don't get tired."

"Sure they do. Mine get sore from holding themselves up all day." She was trying to hook the eye. She made several passes.

"They don't look tired."

She paused a minute to stare, her hands behind her back, her elbows flapping out like wings. She said, "Are you flirting with me?"

"Flirting?" I said. I crossed my arms. "I wouldn't know how." It was the absolute truth.

She began buttoning her blouse. "You mean if you wanted to."

"What?"

"You wouldn't know how, if you wanted to."

"I guess."

She smiled as if she'd won something.

Twenty-three

———

They refused to let Maeve shave for the big mixed meeting, even with supervision. She said she didn't care but
then wouldn't ride the elevator with all the other girls.
She and I took the stairs. She wore the same ruffled blouse
from the day in my room and a skintight flowered miniskirt
that came two inches past her crotch. The hair on her legs
was visible through her smoky hose. The skirt was too tight.
Her stomach showed right through. Not simply the round-
ness that most women have. It was a rope of flesh that
curved above her pubic ridge.

"Like it?" She stopped and twirled on the landing.

I watched my feet descend the stairs, wondering
how she could possibly think she looked good. "You're
ready for spring."

"Ready for something." She dug her elbow in my
side.

It hurt, and I said, "Quit it."

"My, my," she said.

I sulked all the way to the foot of the stairs.

She looked at my oversized chinos and raglan
sweater. "Do you always wear such boring clothes?"

I raised my voice. "Maeve—"

"Boy, someone's on the rag."

"Shut up!"

"Or is that not possible anymore?"

I burst into tears.

Maeve put a guilty arm around me. My chest

heaved. She held on, but loosely. I was really blubbering. When it was over, she wiped my face with the cuff of her blouse.

I said, "My first tears at Seaview, and Gert isn't here to record them."

"I'll tell her for you."

I said, "I hate that expression."

"What expression?"

"On the rag."

"When was your last period?"

"Three years ago. Maybe four. At first, it sort of came and went. I didn't keep track. I don't remember when I realized it was gone for good." I shrugged. "I didn't think I'd missed it."

"Of course you missed it."

"Why do you say that?"

"It's like—it's how we know we're girls."

Just then the men started coming down, slippers and all. We stepped behind the staircase and watched their backs file past. Maeve took my hand. She said, "It's one of the ways."

Inside, we sat in the front row, separate from the other girls. All through the meeting she kept crossing and uncrossing her legs. The guy who told his story was a fireman. He'd done cocaine and booze. He was masculine in a cartoonish way. Clark Kent without the glasses, Superman in jeans instead of tights. Maeve leaned forward while he spoke. He even had a cleft chin. In fifteen minutes, he didn't blink once.

We had a break halfway through. For cigarettes and trips to the john. That's what the men called it, the john. There was only one men's room on the first floor and it was never locked, even though, supposedly, there were men on the eating disorders unit from time to time. Still, they received that courtesy, that gesture of good faith and trust that we girls, apparently, did not merit: an unlocked door. During the break, a nurse stood outside the doors to both.

When I returned from peeing, there was a receiving line to talk to Maeve. Joey R. was telling her about his Sicilian grandmother. Tiny Regular was next. I looked for the tightly wound fireman who'd led the meeting but couldn't find him. Most of my unit was grouped together against one wall. The big-haired bulimic girls wrung their hands. Maeve was the show.

Just before the meeting resumed, Maeve excused herself to the john. We were called to order. Two people shared, then a third. When the next person started talking, I made my way across the room. I told the third-floor counselor who stopped me that I had to change my tampon. He opened the door.

At the women's bathroom I heard funny sounds and thought that Maeve was puking. The nurse was gone. I pushed the door but it was locked. I tried the men's. It gave.

I had never been inside a men's bathroom before and felt instantly ashamed. Three urinals lined the right-hand wall. They looked like men's bodies, all open and exposed. Water gurgled in them. I heard the noise again. Not puking. A row of stalls stood opposite the urinals. I crouched low to look. There was no one inside the stalls. At the end of the row, I spied a pair of Seaview slippers. And a woman's shoe. Maeve's shoe. Trousers fell and covered the slippered feet. I straightened up. I knew I should leave; I wanted to. There was a smell other than the bathroom smell. I covered my mouth and nose. My breath was hot. Maeve's second shoe dropped. My feet carried me to the edge of the last stall. All I had to do was look. They would be too busy to see.

I peered around and was greeted by the bare behind of the fireman who'd told his story. His white undershorts were caught at his thighs; they made his pinkish skin look red. Dark, curly hair ran up and down his legs. Maeve sat on the sink, her knees pressing into his back. His movements lifted her up, then down, up, then down, her bare ass slapping the porcelain. He wore garters. The black elastic gripped the high, hard ball of his calves. Her stockings were ripped, and I could see she wasn't wearing any panties underneath. Just then, I recognized the smell. It was me.

On my way out, my right shoulder slammed a stall door and the whole row rattled. The grunting stopped, but I didn't wait to be discovered. I went straight to my room and climbed into bed, clothes and all. I couldn't concentrate. I tried to hold on to one thought at a time, but they seemed to gather and disperse. I felt panicky. I masturbated, hating it, dreading the emptiness that comes after. Then I cried for the second time that day and fell asleep.

PART

IV

Twenty-four

A t the end of our senior year in high school, Ronald Tillman and I agreed to a mutual deflowering. We'd become friends three years before, while doing a group project on *Wuthering Heights*. For a month, we'd read our favorite passages out loud to each other over the phone before going to bed. We started studying at each other's houses, and I will never forget Syd's surprise when I brought Ronald for the first time through the kitchen into the living room, where she was constantly rearranging things—silk flowers or porcelain figurines or the family pictures on the mantel. That day she had a duster in hand as she repositioned her Hummels, and when she heard our stockinged feet on the white pile carpet—no shoes ever in the living room—she turned around with the yellow feather duster high in the air, near her temple, and smiled enormously at Ronald's unexpected blackness, which was set off in particular relief by Syd's white-on-white furnishings. She waved the duster at us and a cloud of particles flew. I remembered when she'd done the decorating, she'd brought home a book of paint samples; every possible variation of white was included: bone, oatmeal, eggshell, ecru, ivory, antique, cream, buff, alabaster. The irony was, and it struck me right there, in the middle of Syd's discomfort masquerading as enthusiasm, that despite the book of samples, there was only one color white, the white that we were, the white that everyone who we knew in Deer Park was. Syd welcomed Ronald effusively; after settling us in the den to study (one could watch

TV, wear shoes, and eat popcorn in the den), she baked us cookies, something she'd never done before.

Ronald represented many firsts for me: he was my first real friend; he was the first intellectual I knew; he was the first black person with whom I had more than a casual acquaintance; and he took me for my first visit to a Catholic church. Ronald attended adult confirmation classes—his parents believed that children should decide for themselves—and after I expressed interest, he asked his teacher if I could join.

Adult confirmation class was tailored specifically for converts and met every Saturday night in the rectory, where the parish priests lived, which was incentive enough, the possibility of glimpsing the intimate daily lives of the celibate men in black slacks and occasional dresses. The priests were always just turning a corner as I got there. I would stand respectfully in the foyer, removing hat and coat and shoes (they had fragile cherry wood floors and the same rule about footwear as Syd) and, invariably, a rustle of black cassock would twirl away from me around a baseboard. Right after, Ronald would stick his head out of our classroom, where he'd arrived early, and say, "You just missed Father O'Leary. He said a prayer for our studies." Or, "Father Calabrese just blessed our throats." Our class was held in the rectory library, which had a long oak conference table, mission style, and an entire bookshelf devoted to the lives of saints.

The teacher, Sister Geraldine, answered our most difficult questions without flinching. No subject could shake her, not hell and whether our non-Catholic friends would go there, not the Holy Trinity, not transubstantiation. She told one fellow who insisted that the priest was only speaking metaphorically about the body and blood that he better get on over to the Episcopal church if he was interested in metaphor. But her area of special interest, her expertise if you will, was in female saints. She had what seemed like an unlimited supply of saints in her memory, and she punctuated our lessons with anecdotes of female piety and self-sacrifice.

Ronald and I began studying saints in earnest. Sister Geraldine assigned us one-page essays on individual saints, which we read out loud to the whole class. Ronald's and my favorite saints were Perpetua and Felicitas, who'd died in A.D. 203. Like us, they were catechumens, which meant they were studying for conversion, and they were fiercely loyal to each other. Felicitas was eight months pregnant when they were captured and sentenced to be thrown to "wild beasts"; Perpetua was nursing an infant son. Felicitas, who'd confessed her faith freely, was worried only that her condition would prevent her from dying with Perpetua, but luckily gave birth three days before the public games. It said in one of the big saint books with a red cover and embossed lettering on the spine that the pair "joyfully" entered the amphitheater where they were wrapped in a net and delivered to a savage cow. They embraced one last time before being finished off by gladiators. Ronald thought the fact that their friendship had developed across class, if not race, lines—Felicitas had been a slave, while Perpetua was "a woman of position"—was wildly coincidental, although we didn't know if slave status in A.D. 203 made Felicitas Egyptian or Hebrew. He talked heretically (and only half seriously) about reincarnation. In our entire high school correspondence, notes passed in the hall between classes, we used the initials F and P to refer to each other.

On the last day of our senior year, with popular girls weeping in the hallways, clutching yearbooks and wilting carnations, and voke-tech boys slamming lockers and letting out earsplitting yells, as if to say, this is *it*, at last, the beginning of *life*, Ronald left me a surprising note using our full saint names.

Perpetua,

Here we are at the threshold of the end of innocence. For you, the pursuit of history at Boston College;

for me, classical studies at Amherst; for us both a jour-
ney toward the ever-widening circle of knowledge that
comes from experience, which is only suffering thought-
fully examined. So off we go, in three short months,
toward passion, suffering, knowledge, and our true
selves, innocents on the precipice of corruption, and I
ask myself how I can possibly leave you—who has
brought me so much knowledge of myself and of others—how I can possibly offer my faithful innocence to
any other?

Felicitas

At first, I wondered why this sudden carnal interest.
Ronald liked to say that we were intimate in every way but
one. We knew the most important things about each other,
things that nobody else knew. He knew about my mother:
her shopping sprees and oppressive femininity, her failed
marriage, invasive hovering, and erratic moods. I knew
about his uptight parents, so intent on not misstepping in
their new white suburb, so focused on Ronald's string of
straight A's, so eager to forget where they had come from.
He knew about my fear of death, which could catch me
unawares, in math class doing theorems, in gym after innocent pushups or leg lifts, a fear that left me panting and
panic-stricken and racing down the hall to find Alex, whose
presence, if not his sympathy, invariably calmed me. I knew
about Ronald's fantasy life, his ability to enter whatever text
we were reading, his complete identification with Heathcliff
and Catherine, with Jane Eyre and Mr. Rochester and his
mad wife, an identification that left him sobbing and spent at
the end of almost every book we read. He knew about—and
first enjoyed, then later came to hate, and ultimately forgave—my initial fascination with his blackness. It was the
hardest of all the things to tell.

So we knew this much about each other, as much,
you could say, as we knew about ourselves. What we didn't
know was what each other's bodies looked like naked.

Whether my nipples were pink or brown, whether his penis curved left or right against his stomach, like Alex's, which I had seen erect only by accident, passing his open door one night as he slept with the covers tangled in a ball at his feet. We didn't know about the electric currents that ran beneath the surface of each other's skin; we didn't know the effect of touch or tongue; we did not know whether it would hurt, whether it would be easy or difficult to maneuver. We wondered aloud about the mysterious rhythm of sex, often alluded to in jokes, and we worried that our bodies might not hear it, might ignore it and never catch on. He admitted to being afraid of not being able to find the opening; I admitted to being afraid of not opening wide enough. I'd heard about girls who experienced so much pain they could not continue; he'd heard about boys who couldn't, not for the life of them, get it in.

We agreed to help each other, to give directions, not to laugh and not to tear my flesh. I was resigned to a certain amount of pain, but we agreed to go slowly. Ronald was in charge of condoms, candles, music; I was in charge of securing a place and bringing towels, or whatever, to deal with the blood. As an added precaution, I borrowed a tube of spermicidal jelly from Syd's dresser.

We planned carefully. There was a weekend in July when Syd was doing est. She was staying at the Park Plaza Hotel in Boston. Ronald and I decided to have sex at my house during the day. This seemed a brilliant strategy. All of the sex we knew about happened at night and in cars, usually by the reservoir or at one of the scenic overlooks on Blue Hill. Neither set of parents would ever suspect daytime intercourse.

He called me that morning. "Everything clear?"

"So far, so good. Syd left at ten. I helped her pack. She took enough clothes for a week."

"Are you sure you want to do this? We don't have to. I want you to know that. I mean, if you change your mind, it's okay."

"No, no, I'm ready. Do you—are you having second thoughts?"

"Oh no. I just thought, well, I wanted to give you an out if you wanted one. I mean, this is different for girls and guys, right? Losing your virginity?"

"I guess."

"I just want to be sure nothing will change. After."

"Nothing will change. At least, not on my part."

"I mean, I just hope we don't have these huge expectations. We're just doing this because we can, because we won't hurt each other, because we're such good friends?"

"Because we're best friends."

"Right. Okay. Good. What time should I come by?"

It was eleven-thirty in the morning. It seemed absurd. "I don't know, what do you think?"

"How about this afternoon. I still have to buy condoms."

"You haven't gotten them yet?"

He sounded embarrassed. "No, I have to go to a pharmacy in Stoughton or Braintree to get them. I can't very well ask my mother's druggist for condoms."

"What if you can't get them?"

"Don't worry, I will. Look, I'll call you from the drugstore when I'm ready to come over."

"You got your mother's car?"

"No. It's in the shop. I'll take the bus."

The bus, I said to myself as I hung up the phone. How prosaic.

Had I been entirely honest then, I would have acknowledged that, despite our closeness, there were still some things Ronald didn't know about me. Things I hadn't shared. We'd talked a lot about very private feelings, about despair, worthlessness, insecurity, but never about emptiness, that hollow, formless *lack* of feeling. Of course, it wasn't as pervasive in high school as it became later, in college and after. And it wasn't exactly as if I were keeping it from him. It was more like I hadn't figured it out yet. The emptiness was related in some way to my fear of death. But it was different too, more degrading. The fear of death, at least, came from outside me.

So I never told Ronald of this emptiness, which I had started to feel, though couldn't quite locate, my last year of high school, and which I felt expand after the one and only time we had sex, frankly and urgently. It made me wonder, when I had the time to wonder, what things Ronald hadn't told.

He arrived around two-thirty, without calling, coming straight from the CVS Pharmacy in Braintree and riding the crosstown bus on which he had been seated next to Mrs. Zapides, the school librarian, who thought he was a genius and who had engaged him in a long discussion about Edith Wharton's *Ethan Frome*. Ronald arrived clutching a brown paper bag.

I was watching television. Reruns of *I Love Lucy*. It was the episode when she and Ethel get stuck working on an assembly line in a chocolate factory. Ronald and I stood in the living room watching Lucy stuff chocolate after chocolate into her mouth, down her blouse, into the square pockets of her worker's smock; her eyes grew wide with panic at the pitilessness of the conveyor belt, at the insidious nature of her own desire. We laughed out loud.

"I can't believe what she can do with her mouth," I said. "It's practically inhuman."

"You have a pretty mouth," Ronald said quietly.

I looked at him. His skin shone with embarrassment. I had never thought of my mouth as having the potential to be pretty. It had, until then, been just a mouth, used for eating, talking. I said, "You don't have to say that. Say things."

"What should we do, then?"

"I don't know." I wished we hadn't watched Lucy. "I just don't want you to make things up."

"I wasn't. You have a pretty mouth."

"How can a mouth be pretty?"

"It just can be, Alice."

"Let's go upstairs."

I had set things up in what was once Syd and Dad's room and now was my mother's solely. She had the only double bed. I'd lowered the shades, brought in my tape player, laid a towel on the bed beneath the covers. The spermicide was on the nightstand, a white tube, already bent and crinkled from use. Syd did not push from the bottom (she and Dad used to have this argument about toothpaste) but from the middle, leaving the tube in the shape of a dilapidated, frowzy bow tie. I could tell from the hard crust of jelly congealed on the cap that it hadn't been opened in a while. Maybe years. I wondered exactly how long.

Ronald went over to the tape player. From the paper bag he drew a cassette of James Taylor. I'd forgotten he had such corny taste.

I sat on the end of the bed.

Ronald walked over to each window, peeked outside the shades.

I tugged at the nubs of the chenille bedspread.

Ronald jammed his hands in his front pockets, looked at me, smiled, and went over to the cassette player. He fast-forwarded through "You've Got a Friend," stopping the tape at "Fire and Rain."

"This is about a girl who dies," I said.

"I know," he said, "it's totally sad." He sang softly, "But I always thought that I'd see you, baby, one more time again." He looked like he was going to cry.

I got up and pulled back the covers, revealing the terry bath towel intended to absorb the excesses of our lovemaking. It felt like we were preparing to wet the bed.

I said, "Something's not right. I don't know."

"Maybe we should go in your room. It's kind of weird being in your mother's, all the lace."

I looked around. Syd had skirted everything with ruffles—the bed itself, a reading chair, the curtains that covered the shades.

"Okay, but let's not leave anything in here."

My room was not much better—the princess bedroom set, complete with vanity, the stuffed animals piled on the single bed that suddenly looked so small, the row of swimming trophies, my noseclip and ear molds—but we got right to business. Ronald set up the tape player, switched to Joni Mitchell, took a candle from the brown paper bag and lit it on my nightstand, although it wasn't a bit dark. He took a package of condoms from the bag. I cleared the stuffed animals off my bed and laid down the towel, tucking one end under the pillow. I pulled the shades.

Ronald said, "Do you have a robe I could borrow?"

I hadn't thought of that. I went across the hall and got an old one of Alex's. Ronald headed toward the bathroom. I took off my clothes as fast as possible—oh, the shame of being caught half dressed—and hurried under the covers. I lay still, listening to water run in the sink. What was he cleaning? His hands? His penis? Was he brushing his teeth? The terry towel felt obtrusive under my skin.

Ronald appeared looking clean and serious in Alex's old red robe. He carried his clothes folded neatly in a pile. He deposited them on my reading chair. He sat on the corner of my bed, facing me, and put his hand on my cheek, almost paternal. When he moved, the robe did too, and I saw a slice of dark brown thigh.

He said, "This is funny."

"Funny ha-ha?"

"Funny strange."

"I know."

I had begun to feel something, though, a stirring, an awareness of what was between my legs. I was beginning to want to do this.

Ronald took a condom from the package on the night table and read the directions on the back of the box. "I got lubricated," he said.

"Good," I said, not knowing the alternatives.

"Ribbed."

"Ribbed? Like a sweater?"
Ronald indicated the box.
"What are ribs for?"
He read: "For maximum pleasure."
"Whose?" I said.
"I don't know. Both of us, I guess."

He slipped off the robe and slid under the top sheet. His collarbones surrounded his neck like the flutes of a fan.

We started kissing—it was the only thing we had any degree of knowledge about—with our hands at our sides, then with them resting lightly on each other's hips. He was the first to use his tongue. It was nice. We were both propped up on our elbows and my hip rose higher than his. The sheet formed a tent around his sex and mine. I could tell without looking, without feeling it against my leg, that he had an erection. With one hand, he fumbled with the condom in its wrapper. I knew I was supposed to help. I was supposed to put the condom on, pull it up (or was it down?), like a sock on a foot, like real rubbers, and I was supposed to smear the jelly—I had read that; it would be erotic instead of medicinal if I smeared the jelly—but then I remembered the jelly was still on Syd's nightstand.

This stopped the show. I had to disengage, pull back, get out of bed—it felt humiliating to grab the robe and it felt humiliating not to—and race naked to Syd's room. The air was cool against my bare skin. I had started to sweat. I snatched up the spermicide and snuck a peek at myself, almost as an afterthought, in the mirror on the back of Syd's bedroom door. I was looking to see if the sex we were about to have had already changed me. Instead I saw the familiar catalogue. I knew it well, had always been a mirror hound like Syd, but today the catalogue of my dissatisfaction insisted itself, meant something more, said, This is all you get, whatever you've imagined for yourself ends here. Hips impossibly wide, flabby stomach, lopsided breasts, narrow shoulders. This is all you will ever be.

I hurried back to Ronald, flung myself in bed, the mattress bouncing shamefully at my sudden weight.

We began again, but I was elsewhere. The early flickers of desire had extinguished themselves in Syd's mirror. We kissed, and Ronald even climbed on top of me, light as a pillow, his persistent, polite erection pressing into me. It curved left—no, right—I was facing him. He reached between my legs and finding utter dryness, asked me what to do.

"How do you mean?"

That's when he asked if I'd ever touched myself before.

I shook my head.

He was surprised.

I was surprised. We'd been confirmed together. We'd sat side by side and learned about sin. I said, "Sister Geraldine said—"

"She said a lot of things, Alice, a lot of things."

It ended up feeling more like work than pleasure. Ronald knew enough, had read enough, to wait until I was ready. He kissed me gently and not so gently, he explored my body with his hands and with his tongue. I watched his face. He was concentrating, dutifully crossing off items on a checklist. I climbed on top of him and felt his penis with my hands, watched his eyelids flutter as I held it, watched his back arch, the bones of his rib cage pushing skyward as I rubbed. I licked the vein. Watched him come. Felt the sticky, off-white liquid on my thighs. Watched him shrivel and inflate again, felt his patience and his insistence and finally lay back and spread my legs to him. It burned going in, not pain like in a rip or a tear, but the fire of an Indian sunburn. Ronald's eyes opened wide in disbelief and excitement, and he pushed farther in, farther in, making room for himself, as far as it would go, his hips tipping daintily. And I thought, There, I'm done, no longer embarrassingly chaste. His body caught the rhythm we had heard about and he seemed to lose himself in the movement, his eyes focused on something over my shoulder, but I could only watch, feeling ugly and awkward, my kneecaps at my temples, my inner thighs straining to stretch wide enough to contain him, my plummy sex exposed to the afternoon air. Like an insect turned indecently on its back, I flailed.

That night we went to the movies. I sat grateful for the dark, eating popcorn, watching Jill Clayburgh being cuckolded by her husband in *An Unmarried Woman,* thinking, But women can't be cuckolded, not linguistically anyway; only men are cuckolds, only husbands can be disgraced by infidelity. Right then I felt the velvet emptiness steal into my stomach, expanding its territory like a river in a flood. I finished our bucket of popcorn and went back for a second. By the end of the week, Ronald and I progressed from awkward conversation to silence. Two weeks later, we went off to separate colleges without speaking. When I arrived at Boston College, I weighed 135. I went on my first diet since junior high school. When I came home for Christmas break, I weighed 117.

Twenty-five

We took Route 139 to 53 to the Hanover Mall. It was a forty-minute drive that took us an hour in the rain. Our windows fogged, and I had to wipe a patch in order to see. It was the second week of April but looked more like February, the yellow grass unable to stand. In places, there was still some snow, oddly sculptured clumps gone black from gravel and exhaust. The rain couldn't seem to melt them.

You had to weigh one hundred pounds (or the equivalent for your height) and be at Seaview at least ten days before you could go to the mall. And you couldn't be on probation. Maeve was on probation, but she talked the counselors into letting her go anyway. She and the fireman were both on probation. They'd gotten caught when the counselor I'd lied to came looking for me. Maeve had spent the entire next day in an emergency meeting with her team and we'd been certain she was going to get kicked out. Louise was the one who told us she wouldn't be. Louise said Seaview was a business, like any other, dependent on its paying customers.

On the minibus, Maeve chose the very last seat. I sat in the next one, my arm dangling over the seat back. Louise and Gwen were across the aisle. Louise wore one of those plastic rain bonnets that collapse into convenient squares. Gwen had on a yellow slicker.

Amy did not sit with us. She had her own group toward the front: Penny, Queen Victoria, a new anorexic, and Penny's exercise friends. They whispered and giggled in great rushes, then shushed each other. Amy kept looking in our direction.

Twenty minutes into the drive, Maeve said, "Story time."

I felt a shiver pass from me to Gwen to Louise. We shifted in our seats. What would she make us do next?

Maeve said, "Louise, how'd you get to Seaview this time?"

Louise was facing out the window, her bonnet tied in a bow beneath her chins. She'd cried twice today, in meditation and then in food group. She looked over at Maeve, her face still puffy, and shrugged.

Maeve said, "Oh, come on. Had to be something special for your parents to spring for a third go-round."

Louise sniffed.

Maeve said, "We could use a story. We've got a ways to go."

Gwen handed Louise a tissue, and Louise blew her nose. Between honks, she said, "I want to tell a different story. I want to answer the question you asked before. About being in love."

"All right," said Maeve. "I guess so." She liked to be in charge of things, even of what we said. "But no Boston Edison, Louise. No telephone repairmen. No invisible friends. I was talking about the real thing."

Louise said, "The real thing."

Maeve sat back and crossed her arms. "Be my guest."

Louise took off her bonnet and shook it dry. Her hair fanned out of its bob, frizzy. It made her face seem smaller. "I was thirteen and not very big yet. I think I weighed less than two hundred pounds."

Maeve snorted.

I had never seen her be mean to Louise. It made me glad—I felt the thrill of her attention turning toward me—but it nagged too. I knew what it implied. I knew that people eventually treated their new friends like the old.

Louise said, "His name was Ray Johnson. He was fifteen. The only Protestant in an all-Jewish development. He mowed lawns on Saturday. He did ours last, and, after, we sat on the porch and talked. I gave him advice about his science project."

Maeve said, "An intellectual affair."

Louise said, "He was studying black holes."

Maeve snorted again.

I tried to gauge the length of her attention span, that is, how long before Maeve got bored and used what she knew against you.

"He wanted to demonstrate their constant movement inward on themselves," said Louise. "My mother had done her doctoral thesis on black holes so I knew all about them. Ray Johnson said I was the smartest girl he knew."

Maeve sat forward. "So he loved you for your mind."

Louise began to fold her bonnet along the pleats. "He whispered, 'Tell me again about singularity.' His breath made my ear feel clammy. He smelled of dry leaves. I said, 'Singularity constitutes the center of the black hole. It is the point at which a massive star falls inward on itself, the crushing weight compressing to zero volume and infinite density."

We were still. It was as if she were reciting a poem.

Louise said, "Ray Johnson marveled at my description of singularity. 'Infinite density.' He said it over and over. And then he took my fingers in his mouth."

Maeve said, "Let's cut to the chase, Louise. Did he find your black hole, or what?"

I winced. She said the most obvious things.

Louise's yes was a hiss. "Two weeks before the Westinghouse finals I stole one of my mother's models for him to copy. He kissed me for the first time, and we went under the porch. He made me keep my clothes on."

"So what happened to him?" asked Maeve.

"Did he ever love you back?" asked Gwen.

Louise said, "He came in second place, got his picture printed in the 'Metro' section of the *Boston Globe*, and I never saw him again. His sister mowed our lawn after that."

And the waterworks came.

Gwen had no more tissues.

For a moment, I hated Maeve.

Twenty-six

The orderly parked the van in a handicapped space. He left the engine running for heat and took out a book to read. Maeve made us leave our coats on the bus. The rain had stopped, but the air was cold. "You'll thank me later," she said. I hadn't noticed the cold when we'd boarded the van at Seaview. Perhaps the excitement of being outside had hidden it. I tried to hold my breath until we got inside but couldn't. I inhaled at the curb. The ice air hurt to swallow.

We entered the Hanover Mall through Jordan Marsh, a big department store. The dozen of us dispersed immediately, our fingers outstretched in a kind of blindman's bluff. We reached for coarse wool sweaters, hard-edged rhinestone jewelry, alligator shoes, fuzzy slippers, handmade soaps, and vinyl pocketbooks. The hospital had so few textures. We must have been easy to spot each week, rummaging indiscriminately.

I felt dizzy. The air was not quite thin, but artificial and controlled in a way different from Seaview's. I smelled perfume, floor wax, cookies baking. The theory behind these weekly furloughs, I understood, was to expose us to real-world temptations—unlimited food and unattended toilets—within the context of the institution, which was embodied by the other patients. In other words, if anyone misbehaved, one of us would squeal.

After half an hour fondling sweaters—I could never

get warm enough—I ran into Maeve at a fragrance counter. A woman in a white lab coat held her by the wrist.

"*Avarice!*" Maeve said. "Take a whiff."

I bent over her forearm.

"Sean asked me to pick up a few things."

"Sean?"

"My fireman friend."

"Oh." Ours was the only unit allowed visits to the mall. The addicts negotiated errands.

"He wants cologne and a five-pound bag of M&M's," she said.

"Isn't that for women?" I pointed to the heart-shaped bottle.

She shrugged. "He said get one for me and one for him."

"Oh."

"That must be your favorite word."

"What's that?"

"*Oh.* You say it all the time."

"Do I?"

Maeve told the woman to wrap the bottle. "It's one of the things I hate most about rehab."

"What's that?"

"Not smelling like me."

I checked another *oh*. Not smelling was what I liked the most. Gwen and Louise came toward us, Gwen walking slowly in order to keep pace with Louise.

Maeve took the test bottle from the counter and gave them each a squirt.

Gwen said, "Nice."

Louise just sniffed, looking hurt. I wondered how long she would stay angry at Maeve. It seemed so unprofitable.

Maeve said, "This is the plan."

We three looked at Maeve. We'd been waiting. Each of us privately waiting. We had known she would have a plan.

"It's two-thirty. We're due back at the van at five. Why don't we go our separate ways and rendezvous, say in an hour and a half, at Friendly's or Brigham's. There's bound to be a Brigham's here."

"There is," I said, almost against my own will. Syd and I had shopped this mall. "It's diagonally across from Filene's."

"Perfect," said Maeve. "I'll see you there at four o'clock. For banana splits." She took her package from the fragrance woman. "Let's synchronize our watches." She roared. We saw the corrugated red roof of her mouth. Seaview had confiscated our watches. Part of their love of control: they said we didn't need to know what time it was, just which group to go to next. Maeve started off. She was wearing harem pants with a matching tunic top. We watched her flounce through the racks of clothes toward the other stores.

I took a step. "I guess I'll see you later." I felt humiliated at having been left with the others. As if Maeve valued us all the same. "Have fun," I said.

Louise inched closer to Gwen.

Twenty-seven

People were hurrying, women mostly, women and small children and retirees were hurrying unconvincingly from store to store, square paper shopping bags slapping against their thighs. Most had not heeded Maeve's advice and still wore their heavy wool coats or down parkas, the hoods trimmed with imitation fur, the zippers unzipped or the buttons undone, exposing lumpy winter shapes. They were sweating underneath the weight of their clothes. Gert had said it was the coldest April in years. A record-breaker.

A giant purple bunny was taking kids on his knee in front of Child World. Young women dressed as Easter eggs handed out jelly beans and coupons to the people in line. No matter that Easter had passed. Parents stood with red-faced children, overheated from their snowsuits. The crankiest ones cried and pulled away from the line, and when their parents bent to pick them up they went slack with resistance, every bit of their tiny bodies in limp revolt.

I remembered once, when I was a kid, having pneumonia and being in an oxygen tent in the hospital. I remembered sneaking out of it at night to pee in private in the bathroom rather than ringing for the nurse and using the dreaded public bedpan. When I climbed out of the tent, I was lightheaded, every surface new, my palms cool and moist. And even at six, in the first grade, I wondered whether this sudden, unfiltered air would support me, sustain my sickly lungs all the way across the cold floor to the

too high toilet and back. I think I held my breath the whole
way. Being in the Hanover Mall was not unlike that. I felt
unprotected. I wanted to walk holding on to things.

Filene's was Syd's preference in the second-tier department stores. I went there because they set them all up
identically, and it would be, at the very least, familiar. And,
of course, Filene's was close to Brigham's. I rode the escalator to the second floor. In Juniors I came upon a glen of
aviator clothes. A blown-up photo of Amelia Earhart stood
propped against a rack of flight jackets. She was grinning,
stepping into a plane. Next to the flight jackets were one-
piece denim jumpsuits.

It occurred to me that Maeve had already lost interest in our friendship, that her attention, though it had
seemed to be coming my way on the bus, was simultaneously waning. After all, she'd dumped the three of us
equally.

How to pass the remaining hour and a half? I'd been
looking forward to the trip all week, and Maeve had ruined
it. Made the fleeting time crawl. I wanted to cry, the third
time in as many days. Another record-breaker. My knuckles
were bone white against the racks of clothes. I considered
eating. I tried to remember the food at this particular mall.
There was one good restaurant. Charley's Something. Or
Something Charley's. The bar part had peanut shells on the
floor. I pictured the heaviest pasta: *tortellini con quattro
formaggio.* More cheese than I'd eaten in a year. It would
land like a soft blow. I came to a rack of suede blouses.
Maeve wore one in forest green. I knew enough not to think
long about the pasta. If I thought too much, it would take
hold.

But an hour and a half! Maybe I would buy a book
and join the orderly on the bus. Lately I'd had trouble reading. I came upon a plaid boutique. Miniskirts and kilts with
giant safety pins. Did anyone look good in these? Amy, I
supposed. If I was honest with myself—and if we were

taught anything at Seaview, we were taught to be honest with ourselves—what I really wanted was to shop for Maeve.

She'd bought herself perfume. That left me what? Lipstick? Eye shadow? A hairbrush? I knew enough to get something for her body. Hosiery? A nightgown? Then it dawned. A new bra. The one I had seen had tears along the seams. I passed plaid stretch pants, lumberjack coats, tartan socks and tams en route to the escalator. When I slipped my foot onto the rising metal slats, it occurred to me that it might look strange, me buying Maeve a bra. I wondered what Louise and Gwen would say. I grabbed the rubber handrail. The metal slats fitted together to form a stair beneath my feet. My black loafers teetered over the edge. I said out loud, "You have a crush on Maeve." Two teenagers riding the escalator in the opposite direction stared.

I rode past lingerie and got off at toys and housewares. There were clocks on every wall. Not yet three. Still more than an hour to go. I kept walking. I came upon a huge display: Barbie's Retrospective. Mattel was celebrating her twenty-fifth birthday. They had black Barbie, Chinese Barbie, Malibu Barbie, gymnast Barbie. And all the habitats: Barbie's supermarket, her Golden Dream Motor Home, and bedroom. There was even a Barbie Mustang.

I tried to remember crushes I'd had on girls. Maeve wasn't the first. Girls had crushes on girls. Everyone knew that. It was universal, like being afraid of the dark. I remembered Syd had teased me about the grade-school teachers I'd liked. Miss Clooney. Miss Gleason. My favorite, Mrs. Powers. I'd cried one day at Old Silver Beach when she and her husband showed up. She had once been Miss Flemings: I took note of the change, but hadn't pictured how or why. He was completely covered with hair, which I'd never seen before. Alex had said "Nice sweater" when the husband happened by. After lunch, she came over to our blanket to say hello, but I couldn't look at her.

Syd called me fickle, right there, in front of everyone. I was being coy, she said. It was the first time I'd heard the word. It was onomatopoeic: coy sounded like how I felt.

I decided to get presents for Gwen and Louise as well.

Twenty-eight

———————

The Filene's girl was busy ringing up purchases. But Mattel had sent a Barbie representative along with the display. She was young enough to have played with Barbie, but old enough to be someone's mother. I guessed her daughter had just started school. This was the first job postmotherhood. I watched her sell an elderly man accessories. Six pairs of plastic high-heeled shoes—pastels. She was enthusiastic and well rehearsed. When I approached, she asked if I had played with Barbie as a child.

I shook my head. "But I have this friend." I figured Louise was too fat a kid to have played with girlish things. Why practice at what you can never be, not in the fullest sense of what it means to be a girl. Which starts with being recognizable in your body.

The Mattel representative looked at me the way counselors must when someone says "I have a friend who has this problem." Her lips parted. She picked the standard Barbie from a row of carbon copies. No two were dressed alike. She opened the box, and said, "Most women in their twenties prefer the original." She winked without moving her cheek, just the lid dropping down. She meant the different-race Barbies were not the same thing. Not the ideal. Of course, she was right: a standard of perfection is, by definition, singular. But it made me uncomfortable. What it implied.

I said, "Are they absolutely identical?"

"I don't know about you," she said, holding up the

doll, "but I see something different in each face. Her expression is—what do you call that?—ironic."

I looked at the familiar, vacant stare, the child's nose.

She opened another box. "And this one. She looks sad around the mouth."

I stared at the cherry-painted lips.

The Mattel rep opened three more Barbies, dropping the empty boxes at our feet, propping the dolls back on the shelf until all five stood in a line, like pageant contestants. She named each of their distinctions.

"Which is your favorite?" I asked.

She puckered her brow, considering. "Mm. It would have to be this one." She indicated Lifeguard Barbie, who was wearing a bright orange bathing suit and a whistle around her neck. "She reminds me of my younger sister. A little tomboyish, but still feminine."

I smiled. "I'll take her."

"Wonderful." She bent to retrieve a box.

The thing I noticed about lying was that it was a practical means of demonstrating disdain. It was a rush. I pointed to the last doll on the left. "I remember the evening gown."

"I thought you said you didn't have her?"

"The girl down the street played with Barbie. And those high-heeled shoes. The ones without a back."

"Mules."

I nodded and handed her Syd's American Express card.

On the first floor, I headed toward cosmetics. I was feeling better. Less inconsequential. I wanted something for Gwen's wispy hair. A fancy comb. Tortoiseshell. Or a clasp to hold it up. It had been looking wild lately.

I stopped at each counter: Lancôme, Clinique, Revlon. The women in white lab coats kept coming over. Could they help me? They had hard but miraculous faces, their skin pulled along invisible wires that were tied somewhere behind their ears. Each of their names, prominently displayed on a Filene's badge, ended in a vowel: Bobbi, Veronica, Mindi. The woman at the hair care counter was Zoë.

"I'm looking for a gift for a friend with extremely fine hair. Your length. Something that will hold it back or up."

Zoë nodded and began assembling a stack of possibilities. Her own hair was quite flat, an industrial magenta. She kept it off her square, flat face with two ivory barrettes. There was something don't-mess-with-me about her. She had drawn in her own eyebrows.

She piled up fine-toothed combs, the kind that hold back half a head of hair, plastic and cloth headbands, multicolored barrettes made to look like heavy-duty paper clips, and old-fashioned bone hairpins that women stick through their buns. The last item was a toothy headband. It was imitation tortoiseshell, a half-inch circular strip with the bounce and bite of an accordion. Zoë said it could be worn as a conventional headband, just behind the temples, or doubled over to tie up ponytails. The main thing was, its zigzag teeth grabbed your hair.

"Perfect," I said. "Can I see some other colors?"

"It's mostly just the tortoiseshell."

"But there are variations?"

Zoë blinked and brought out a half dozen.

The differences were subtle. Chaotic swirls of red, brown, and tan. I asked to see more. Zoë seemed genuinely surprised. She left the first six on the counter. I refused the next four she presented. I said, "I have something very particular in mind."

"Apparently."

I accepted the fifth, the darkest brown she'd shown. Zoë all but snatched it from my hand. When she turned to face the cash register, I snuck another band up my sleeve.

Totally unexpected. I hadn't planned to.

She said, "Will that be cash or charge?"

I said, "Filene's charge," and began to pretend-search my clothes. "It must be here."

She sighed before she even turned around. "I've already rung it in."

"I'm awfully sorry."

She faced about. "If you go upstairs to the credit office, they will give you a temporary card that you can use today. That is, if you're a regular card member."

"I am."

"I'll hold this for you. But you have to come right back."

I promised. "What floor is the credit office on?"

Zoë held up four fingers.

When I was a little girl, I was afraid of escalators, especially getting on and off. Syd would rail about the dangers of untied shoelaces, but even wearing my sharpest Mary Janes, I thought the escalator would suck me in, toes first. I pictured myself squashed between those metal slats, appearing and disappearing endlessly. Now I thought about retribution. Sister Geraldine had said no sin went unpunished. I wondered when Zoë would count the headbands. I'd stolen something! It was twice the rush of lying, like going without food for three or four days straight, only accelerated. It had its own forward motion. Maeve would be pleased. I'd get her gift this way.

At lingerie, I picked out every lacy thirty-eight D in black that I could find. I stuffed two bras down the back of my pants, then presented the remaining eight to the fitting room attendant. She was young, slim, and nondescript, a high school student making extra cash. I felt surprisingly unafraid of getting caught; I had years of good behavior written on my face, embedded in the way I moved. The attendant counted the bras and handed me a little plastic number eight. Her hands were red and chapped, the nails bitten back to the skin. She kept glancing from the clump of black brassieres to my sweatered, pancake chest. I chose the farthest dressing room. I was breathing hard.

Inside the dressing room, I took the headband from my sleeve and opened Barbie's box. I slipped the band under

Barbie's feet and returned the box to the big Filene's bag. On second thought, I reopened the box and took out Barbie. She was tied to a piece of cardboard. I bit the white thread that held her arms and legs in place, tasting familiar plastic. I had lied more than once to Miss Mattel. As a girl I'd had Barbie, Julia, and Growing Up Skipper, whose hair length you could change by pressing a button on her back and pulling the strawberry hair straight out the top of her head.

I pulled down Barbie's bathing suit. This was something we did every day as girls: compromise our dolls. The hair-free, nippleless breasts were oddly reassuring. Forever firm. I scissored her legs and ran a finger along the lipless crotch. Who'd thought of this for us? I pulled up the suit and sat Barbie on the bench beside Maeve's bras. I took off my sweater and shirt.

The first of the eight bras was scratchy, a black Dior with skinny silk straps. I couldn't manage the clasp behind my back; I had to close it in front, then yank the bra around. The straps fell loose against my shoulders. I ran my hands down the front of my chest, the way I'd seen Maeve do it. The ridge of the underwire felt like an extra rib. I put on the remaining nine bras, one right on top of the other. Then my shirt, just to see. To imagine me this way.

What struck me was how far apart they were, as if they weren't a pair but separate units. I could fit my fist between them. I thought of Mrs. Wallach, the saleswoman at Innuendos, where Syd had brought me to shop for my first bra. Mrs. Wallach had a bosom, not breasts, a single shelf that jutted out from her squat body. I took the shirt off and stripped down to one bra, the Dior, the most ornate, each piece of lace in the shape of a rose petal. And the most uncomfortable. I snuck my hands under the wire and held my breasts. My hands felt cool against the itch. It was the kind of discomfort you could live with; it told you what was where. I would steal this bra for Maeve. My nipples were hard as beans.

I got dressed again. Button-down shirt and crewneck

sweater over the brassiere. I stuffed one down the back of my pants and assembled the rest. I returned Barbie to her box. The high school girl took my plastic number eight and counted the bras without looking up.

I said, "Do you know the time?"

She held out her watch. It was five minutes past four. One of her cuticles had started to bleed.

"I'm late," I said, and she nodded. I could see her wanting to evaporate. She was easy to picture at Seaview in a year or two. On the way out, I took the last bra from the back of my pants and dropped it on a sale table. I rode the elevator down to the mall level, so as not to run into Zoë.

Twenty-nine

———

I got presents." I said. The three of them were already there, squinched into a padded vinyl booth at Brigham's. I wanted to tell them every piece of it, even the salesgirls.

"You're late." Maeve was peeved.

I said, "Just ten minutes. Besides, I stole you each a present."

"You stole?" They all said it at once.

"Well, two gifts out of three," I said.

"Why?" said Louise.

"I don't know. It just came over me."

Maeve smiled. She said, "Where's the loot?"

I took Barbie out of the cardboard box. There was a general sucking in of breath. I slid next to Maeve. Louise sat diagonally across from me, jammed into the corner. Gwen had less than half a seat. I handed the doll to Louise. "I thought you'd like her."

She held Barbie by the neck. "I never had her." She did not seem pleased.

I said, "She's twenty-five years old. Same age as me."

Louise just stared, no recognition, no thank-you. I was surprised how much it hurt my feelings.

Gwen said, "Can I see?" She held Barbie like a piece of glass, her spindly fingers curved around the waist. She said, "I used to make all her clothes." Gwen bent Barbie's hips and knees and set her on the table.

Louise was spoiling my surprise. I hated that she couldn't be gracious.

Maeve said, "Let's see the rest."

I pulled the headband out of the box.

Gwen knew immediately that it was for her. "It's my favorite kind," she said, her hands flying across the table.

"I wasn't sure," I said.

Gwen felt the accordion points. "They're the best for fly-away hair."

Maeve said, "Put it on."

Gwen shook her head. "Not here." She reached back to smooth her braid. A waitress came over and put down four paper place mats. I asked for water.

Maeve inched me out of the booth and stood. "Why the fuck not? I'll do it."

"It's a restaurant," said Gwen. "There's food."

Maeve took the headband out of Gwen's hands. "It's an ice cream parlor," she said. "It's Brigham's."

Gwen could not have been more bird. Her neck and shoulders folded. She was body and head, no bleached white throat, no delicate collarbone. She covered her hair with both hands.

"Come on," said Maeve. "Think of all the trouble Alice went through." She removed Gwen's hands and began to undo the knotty French braid. Gwen closed her eyes. Louise and I watched Maeve work.

The waitress came back with silverware, and Maeve ordered two banana splits. I said, "How about that water?"

Louise said, "Maeve, what'd you do to your hair?"

I looked up. Louise was right. Maeve had had something done.

Maeve said, "Just a trim." She raked her fingers through Gwen's skim-milk hair.

But there was more. Maeve was wearing different makeup. Her teeth looked brighter. I said, "What else?"

"Lord and Taylor had an all-in-one. Facial. Manicure.

Pedicure. Totally luxurious. I love when they wedge the cotton between your toes."

Liberated from its braid, Gwen's hair stood every which way.

Maeve said, "I thought it was all one length."

Gwen said, "Let me."

"How come it's all in patches?"

Gwen said, "I'd rather."

Maeve said, "Suit yourself." She sat back down, pushing me farther into the booth. Now I faced Louise. Gwen hurried to the bathroom.

Maeve said, "It always looks so neat in that braid, but really it's a mess."

I said, "That must have cost a fortune."

"What?"

"The all-in-one."

"Sean sprung. The last thing was ten minutes of tanning."

Louise said, "You know that causes cancer."

Maeve shrugged. "Beauty is a duty."

I liked her least like this. I said, "Did Sean order a make-over to go with his M&M's?"

"Frankly, Sean doesn't think anything needs to be made over," said Maeve. "And besides, he doesn't order."

Louise said, "Who's Sean?"

Before Maeve could answer, the waitress arrived with two banana splits, one chocolate, one vanilla. She set them in the middle of the table with four long-necked silver spoons. Louise moved Barbie against the wall.

I said, "Excuse me. I asked for water?"

The waitress wiped her hands on her brown-and-pink-smudged apron. Her eyes fell on the areas where my clothes didn't cover—my veiny wrists and neck. She said, "Water. Right. Coming up."

I could not remember the last time I had been so close to a banana split. The cherry stained the whipped cream red. The nuts had spilled. It all smelled faintly chemical.

Maeve said, "Who wants to share the chocolate one with me?"

Louise and I looked at each other.

Maeve said, "I'm sure Gwen's vanilla all the way." She dipped her spoon into the boat-shaped dish of chocolate.

Just then, Gwen returned, her hair retied in the familiar French braid, the new headband still in hand. "Alice, I just didn't have enough time. Tomorrow I'll wear it. I promise."

"Don't feel you have to," I said. "I just thought—"

"But I love it," she said, sitting next to me. "I really do." She patted my hand.

"Me too," said Louise. "I mean, thank you. Thank you for Barbie. Thank you for thinking of me."

I looked over at Louise. "You're welcome." Something inside me loosened. I smiled. She smiled back. I said, "So what did you do this afternoon?"

Louise and Gwen exchanged looks.

Maeve said, "The ice cream's melting."

Louise stared at the banana split. She said, "I sat on one of those islands in the middle of the mall and tried not to eat."

I'd never in my life felt sorry for fat people. They made choices, just as I did. But I couldn't fathom Louise's lack of self-control. It seemed a life bereft of pleasure. Abnegation masked as indulgence. It made me sad. I said, "So you didn't shop?"

Louise nodded. "We shopped. First thing. Then we sat." She pointed at two large bags underneath the table. "Hickory Farms."

At last the waitress returned with four clear glasses pressed against her chest. She bent way over to set them down and we could see her paltry cleavage. I drank two glasses.

Maeve looked under the table. She said to Louise, "What's in the bags?"

"Pork products."

Maeve licked her spoon. "Come again."

Louise said, "Farm foods. Smoked sausage. Honey-cured ham. Bacon."

Maeve said, "Louise, you're Jewish. Do you even like this stuff?"

"Not really. That's why I bought it."

We sat in silence. Gwen and Louise and I shared the two remaining waters while Maeve finished the chocolate banana split. I didn't think it was possible to eat ice cream noisily, but she did. The vanilla one melted, leaving a reddish yellow puddle around the silver boat. The waitress wiped it up, going back twice to rinse and moisten her rag, each time glancing at one or the other of us.

When we were ready to go, Maeve turned to me. "So where's mine?" She said this with a kind of confidence that meant she knew I'd saved the best for last.

I thought of pretending I'd no gift for her. But even as I thought it, she read my face and smiled. I said, "Close your eyes."

She used one hand to cover them.

I slipped both hands behind my back to unhook the best-for-last Dior. Louise and Gwen looked puzzled. I reached up under my sleeve until I found a strap. When was the last time I'd sneaked off a bra like this? I pulled the first strap over my wrist and freed the other. "You can open."

At first Maeve didn't say a word. Then just "Alice." She held the lace between two fingers.

I said, "D'you like it?"

Maeve hooked the back clasp and held it up for everyone to see. It kept its shape, stiff with wire and well-knit lace.

Gwen mouthed *lovely*. Louise nodded.

I watched the phantom bosom turn and bow.

She said it again, "Alice," and leaned across the table to kiss me on the lips. Not a sister's kiss. I tasted chocolate.

"It's time to go." I stood.

Maeve said, "They haven't given us the check."

I said, "I'll get it." Gwen rose to let me out.

I found our waitress with a family of five. They were ordering bacon cheeseburgers and Diet Cokes. She was annoyed by my interruption and made me stand and wait until she'd recorded every variation from medium to rare. I wanted to say, It doesn't matter, they cook it however they like, but didn't. The family stared. They all had freckled faces. The littlest boy whispered a question to his mother; still looking at me, she whispered back. When the waitress finally tore our check from her pad, it ripped in two and I went voluntarily to the cashier for tape. I took deep breaths all the way to the front of the restaurant and didn't mind the greasy air. At this point, air was air.

I realized that what I wanted from Maeve wasn't physical. I didn't want to touch her. I didn't spend my day thinking about her sexual parts, her lips or breasts or behind. And I didn't fantasize about doing specific things like kissing or groping. My desire for Maeve was more like a dress you want intensely. It's not the thing itself, it's what it will do for you. I wanted what she did for me.

It was a relief to know.

When I got back to the table, she said we had one more stop to make.

I said, "What time is it? It must be getting late."

Maeve pulled Louise's bags out from under the table and handed one to me. "Don't worry. It won't take long."

Louise paid the bill. She was the only one of us with cash.

Thirty

Maeve carried the heavier bag. Mine had mostly accessories to the meat—crackers, bread, jars of baby cornichons. Still, I felt its weight pull against my elbows. I pressed it to my chest with both arms. We walked quickly. It was a lot of walking for one day, and I was tired. My knees ached. Lord and Taylor stood square and white in the distance; I assumed that was our destination. Maeve was, in some small but significant way, going to make us over. We passed the Easter Bunny. Gwen stayed with Louise, who couldn't keep up. The mall was less depressing with Maeve. We passed an imitation Big Ben clock. It said four thirty-five.

I said, "We'll miss the bus."

Maeve laughed. "They'll wait. What's he going to do, fucking leave without us?"

"He might."

Maeve threw her free arm around me. She was a toucher, whoever was in reach, it didn't matter. "He'd lose his job. Relax."

Gwen ran up to us. "Louise says she hopes we're not going to one of those tanning places. She says she burns."

"I bet she does," said Maeve.

"So do I," said Gwen. "Burn."

"I'm not surprised. Look, don't worry. We're not going for a tan."

I said, "Where are we going?"

"We're going to get you a present. Everyone else has

one. We can't leave without finding something for you. It wouldn't be fair."

Gwen dropped back to tell Louise. In the end, it was not Lord and Taylor, but right next door. A bridal boutique, Nell's of Boston. Maeve squeezed my arm. I couldn't get my mouth to close. I'd forgotten Nell's had a store at the Hanover Mall. Gwen and Louise caught up. Between breaths, Louise said, "Here?"

Nell's front windows were filled with old-style mannequins posed in a wedding scene. Inside, the floor was covered with deep purple shag carpet and two facing walls were mirrored. Every image duplicated itself. I watched our foursome multiply. In each version, our bodies stayed exactly the same. I was still the thinnest one.

A saleswoman approached us immediately. She was wearing a handsome beige cocktail dress. Her eyes slid to our bags of food. I wished we hadn't carried them. She gestured with both hands to her own elegant body, and said, "For an informal evening wedding, mother of the bride or important guest." She looked familiar. I tried to remember if Syd and I had been in this particular store. "Now what can I do for you?" She kept looking at the food. "You're not mothers of the bride." She laughed.

Maeve laughed with her. She put down her bag. "No, we're not."

The woman brought her hands together, making the steeple of a church. "Where's the bride?"

Maeve took the Hickory Farms bag out of my hands and put it on the shag carpet next to hers. She pushed me forward. "Alice is the bride. I'm the maid of honor. These two"—she gestured to Gwen and Louise, who were trying not to show Maeve's lie on their shocked faces—"are bridesmaids. It's going to be a snowball wedding."

The saleswoman listened carefully.

Maeve said, "Plunging everything on everyone. We're going to be showing a little flesh. Something daring for Alice. Not the same old dress that every bride will be wearing. Nothing touches the floor. No veil, no train, no petticoats. We want to see her."

"Of course you do," said the woman. "And so you should." She smiled. "But the most we can do today is make an appointment. All fittings are done by appointment only."

I turned to go. Maeve stopped me. "Why's that?"

The woman intensified her smile. She flexed the fingers of the steeple. "We start with the undergarments, the foundation first. Then we work our way up to the actual dress. Miss, er, the bride will have to get fitted for a brassiere as well. One doesn't buy a wedding dress the way one buys a pair of jeans."

"Of course not," said Maeve, her smile brilliant and ingratiating. "Can I speak with you a moment?" They walked together to the opposite end of the store. Maeve put her arm around the saleswoman. Louise and Gwen and I watched them in the mirrors. I remembered her now. She was one of the few salesladies who hadn't liked Syd. She'd thought my mother was too demanding.

When they returned, the woman's face had softened. "Well, if you just want to get a preliminary idea," she said. "I don't see why not."

The dressing rooms were big, with space enough for chairs. Maeve and I fit comfortably in one, Louise and Gwen the other. An attendant worked with them while the beige woman handed dresses to Maeve, who handed them to me.

I whispered, "What'd you say to her?"

Maeve shrugged. "You know. Just that it would really mean a lot."

"Come on."

"I told her it was life and death."

"Who's life?"

"What does it matter. I got you here, didn't I? Now get out of those clothes."

Maeve helped me on and off with everything. I couldn't help but think of the legions of saleswomen who'd looked the other way while I'd tried on dresses for Syd. They were always recommending high necks. We settled on the fifth one, a forties-looking dress, completely off the shoulder, close-fitting but not clingy, and three-quarter length. The skirt flared a bit at the knees. The dress had an edge. Not nice little girl. Maeve said "This is it" before zipping it up.

I said, "I think so too."

"Let me see."

I turned and smiled.

She took a step back. "Fabulous. Keep turning."

I saw myself spin in the dressing room mirror. I looked happy. Maeve saw it too. When I came around, she pulled me to her. I could feel the hardness of my bones against her body. She was huge and plush. I felt a pain between my legs. As if I were opening.

I pulled back a little. I said, "I'm not sure you understand."

"What don't I understand?"

"It's not a physical desire. I don't . . . I mean, I want what you do for me. The way I might want a dress that sets off my color."

"You don't have any color to set off, Alice."

"You know what I mean."

"Explain it to me again."

"I don't know how else to say it. I want what you do for me. What you make possible."

"And what exactly do I make possible?"

"I don't know. Everything. This. Being here. A different life than the one I'd planned."

She loosened her grip. She said, "And you'd planned?"

"I can't say. It's more like I've planned what I don't want rather than what I do. It's been a process, mostly, of elimination."

Maeve released me altogether. "Jesus, Alice. Are you going to spend your whole life this way?"

"What way?"

"Sexually anorexic."

"What's that supposed to mean?"

"You have the same relationship to people that you have to food."

The saleswoman knocked on the door. "How are we doing?"

"Fine," I practically shouted. "Just another minute."

To Maeve I said, "Are you bisexual?"

"Not technically."

"No?"

"It's just. I put anything in my mouth that I can."

I didn't know where that left me.

She said, "But you can relax. I only sleep with girls whose tits are bigger than mine."

I said, "Well, that must narrow it down."

"Fuck you," she said. And we both laughed.

I felt relieved.

"Go on." She gave me a shove. "Beat it. Go show the others."

I stumbled out. In the main salon, my reflection reverberated against the walls. There were purple patches on my face and neck. Gwen and Louise stood holding backless satin dresses. I was amazed at how much they went along. They couldn't know what any of this meant. Gwen came over and felt the fabric of my dress. *Exquisite*, she mouthed.

"You're both being sports," I said.

Gwen told me they hadn't tried anything on: the bridesmaid dresses barely covered Louise. So they'd held them up against their bodies and settled on an antique white satin with a gaping back plunge and a giant bow just above the bum. Something neither of them would ever wear.

I said, "They're perfect."

Maeve came noisily out of our dressing room, wearing the same dress in her size. The beige woman must have given it to her. She trailed after Maeve, excited. After all these ugly weddings, here was someone who could wear a dress! She grabbed a pair of combs from one of the attendants and quickly arranged Maeve's hair on the top of her head. The mirror caught the cream white vee of her back, the curving spine, the hint of ribs, the hollow above the jutting tailbone above the crack in her voluptuous rear. And when she turned, her sides, the sharp outline of breast. Maeve walked over to Louise and took her hand. We fell in line in front of one of the mirrored walls. A pretend wedding party.

I couldn't believe how nice it was. The four of us admiring each other. Imagining normal lives. I got lost there, in Maeve's vision, in the possibility of things.

And then something strange happened: Gwen fell. For no reason we could see. She didn't trip on her dress; she didn't misstep. One second she was looking back at us in the mirror, smiling. The next instant, she was down. And she didn't fall forward or back; she didn't fall to one side. She went straight down. Like a building being demolished, she caved in on herself.

PART

V

Thirty-one

Most of us started getting better after the trip to the mall, which became a mythic event in my memory of Seaview, every other incident divided into *before* and *after* our ride to Hanover. They put us on probation, officially for returning late to the bus, unofficially for the scene at Nell's. Maeve got double probation. The new restrictions were not exactly clear. We were denied privileges that were formally forbidden but informally allowed. Smoking, visiting each other's rooms, reading after ten P.M. Maeve was no longer allowed to leave our floor unescorted.

We all slowed down. Louise stopped eating my dinner or anybody else's. She ate her own meals haltingly and was usually the last to leave the cafeteria. When she did get up to clear her empty plate, you could see her sadness. Not the easy tears from before; it was a dry, aging grief that pinched her face. Maeve was puking less. She said it was only because they had gotten better at catching her, but she seemed genuinely tired of the subterfuge and ruined purses. Friday nights she still purged before the big mixed meeting. She said she liked to feel empty for the boys.

I began eating more food. Thirty-two chews before each swallow. Mostly I got tired of swimming upstream. My vigilance flagged in the face of theirs: Gert's insipid smile, the confidence of the lunchroom ladies, the *atta girls* when I ate my roll. It was too heroic a task to continue on my course. I told myself it didn't matter; I would get out, eventually, and could reaffirm my faith in deprivation.

The first time I cleaned my plate, Maeve and Louise pretended not to notice. They maintained a ridiculously animated discussion about an ex-boyfriend of Maeve's whom Louise had met last time in rehab. Maeve kept leaning far out over the table to touch Louise, the usual tugs and taps, and she inadvertently dragged her breast through mashed potato. I had already eaten every bite of mine. I covered my barren plate with a paper napkin. Dinner had been chicken potpie. The yellow-brown gravy made veins along the ceramic dish. There was a lone mushroom, flat and purplish, the black edges curling like human skin. I brought everything to the stacking area. It was like one of those dreams in which the stalls in the public bathroom don't have doors.

Gwen had osteoporosis. They told us two days after the mall. She was taken by ambulance to Medical, and I had the déjà vu you get when remembering an experience that's only been described to you. (My heart attack was Syd's story, not mine.) They told us Gwen had the bones of a much older woman. Her left hip had cracked in two, the weight of her slender body too much for its porous skeleton. It was hard to take in. They had to tell us twice. They called an assembly, all three floors plus the nurses and shrinks and two doctors from Medical. We crammed into the lecture hall. One of the doctors, a woman with unexpectedly yellow teeth, used diagrams to explain how women lose bone density when they stop bleeding. I remembered that much from Syd's premature ovarian failure. Her early menopause had meant milk with every meal. The danger for old ladies, the doctor at Seaview explained, was not that they'd fall and break a hip, but that they'd break a hip and fall. Gwen's seven years without her period meant seven years of calcium depletion. She was as brittle as sun-dried sticks. As if a drought had baked her bones.

Louise asked if we could visit. Gert said no. There were mild objections, raised hands, a murmuring of protests easily subdued. The truth was, we were afraid to go.

Hank was called in, along with Gwen's parents, to

discuss more intensive treatment options. They met with Gwen's team on the first floor on a Friday afternoon. We caught sight of him on our way to the gym. Hank had promised visits but had never come. He was not homely or frail, as I had figured oboe players, but clean-cut and athletic. Maeve said he looked the type that fooled around but never got caught because he seemed so priggish. He did not look musical. But Louise said she thought he was nice. They passed in the hall that day, and Hank recognized Louise from Gwen's letters. They started talking. When she asked him how Gwen was, he burst into tears.

The very next day, we got a note from Gwen, hand-delivered by Nurse, who walked all the way from Medical with no other purpose. There were kittens playing with a ball of red yarn on the front of the card. It said: "Everybody—Doing intravenous suppers and hormones galore. About every hour, it seems, a lovely glass of milk. Resting easy with the new hip. Missing all of you. Don't fret. Be good.—Gwendolyn."

What worried me was that the doctor said there was no way of replacing bone density once it was lost, our daily calcium pills notwithstanding; it was simply a matter of not losing more.

Life went on at Seaview, though we all wanted it to stop, wanted it to register the loss of Gwen, which, however temporary, loomed large. But the counselors wouldn't pause, or couldn't, in their merciless pursuit of our private, innermost lives. They let us talk about Gwen, but they didn't let us linger. I could see their dilemma with Maeve. Gwen was the first thing she truly went on about. After the first few days, they curbed her monologues about osteoporosis and tried to turn the conversation back to Maeve. This infuriated her.

Despite our indiscretions at the mall, my team was talking about lifting the moratorium on Syd and the possibility of family therapy. I weighed one hundred and eight. Louise's professor parents had agreed to come in for family therapy, and she had lost twenty-eight pounds. Queen Victoria had gotten released. We saw the grandkids in the car on the day her family came to claim her. Cass let us wave from the group room window. Amy said she was scheduled to leave two weeks from Tuesday. No one believed her. Every couple of days, there were new faces. I didn't bother to learn them.

Maeve threw herself into a romance with Sean. She had two official strikes against her. One more, they said, and she was out. She didn't seem to care, which made me wonder who was paying for her hospitalization. She never talked about her family, not even in group therapy. The romance was pretty tame, mostly passing notes and holding hands at the Friday night meeting. Whenever the counselors looked away for long enough, Maeve and Sean made out. It was something to do. The staff determinedly ignored them. Since Maeve wasn't allowed to leave the unit without an escort, I was the principal courier of notes. Which was what I wanted, Maeve's attention without her pursuit. This way, I didn't spend my waking hours counting every girl or boy I'd ever smiled at. I didn't worry about my feelings for her or about our embrace in the dressing room at Nell's. Evidently, neither did Maeve. Seduction was just her way with people; it didn't mean anything. My own crush melted into friendship, the usual course. People commented on our closeness. Gert said we were thick as thieves. I was tremendously relieved.

We looked for ways of measuring time. The days had a sameness. Especially since we were forbidden the mall, even the weekends were repeats. Art class was the place where we could really see our progress, or if not progress, at least the length of our stays. Louise had been the first to finish, although Cass didn't accept her work. Louise completely colored in her drawing, every inch black. She'd used up all the black crayons. Cass told her it wasn't finished.

"But there's nothing more I want to add to it," Louise said reasonably, as if addressing a simple question of aesthetics.

"None of us are single planes, dear," Cass said. "It needs contours, texture. I don't want to see it again until it's fuller, layered. Try. Let your imagination go."

At first Louise just stared at the body outline, the way she stared at her meals. Then one day she asked Cass for a nickel and began scratching a pattern in the black crayon. She wouldn't tell any of us her plan. She'd lost enough weight to work comfortably on the floor. She covered three-quarters of her blackened form with a second sheet of paper and worked on one quarter at a time, lying directly on top of the drawing. This way we couldn't see what she was doing and she protected her clothes from the ubiquitous black crayon curls.

Maeve's figure was the furthest from completion. She was using papier-mâché to create a realistic, if exaggerated, replica of her body. There was something carnival about it. Wild colors for her flesh: reds, purples, greens. She did one body part at a time, first fashioning the papier-mâché, then painting it. I would have done all of the papier-mâché first and painted after. But Maeve insisted on seeing how each part looked before continuing, as if she lacked faith in the whole, and wanted proof at every step before investing more. Limb after limb, it assembled itself.

After days of inactivity, I had decided to render my body, as accurately as possible, without its skin. Cass had ruined my first impulse—stacks of nimbus, cirrus, and cumulus clouds. I had just sketched the outline of my first cloud, a filmy cirrus in place of the features of my face, when Cass felt compelled to mention a former student who had done very successful clouds. She said it like a simple point of information, as though it wouldn't bother me, not being unique. I was stymied for days. Then I had what Cass called a "breakthrough." I asked to borrow an anatomy book from Medical. She said she preferred imagination to accuracy. I concentrated on the cardiovascular system. If I closed my eyes, I could still see the graphs and charts from cardiac care, the prominent pink heart and miles of muscular red wire. I asked for paints and brushes.

And every night in my dreams, I watched Gwen fall.

Thirty-two

Sean got discharged. It was a bit of a surprise. He was supposed to be in for twenty-eight days, but at the last minute his insurance reneged (they had paid for previous rehabilitations) and he had to leave right away, after only twenty-one. He told a friend to tell me when I appeared with Maeve's next note. By the time I got the news to Maeve, he'd been out of the building for five hours.

At first she seemed mostly bothered by the fact that she'd been taken by surprise. She'd felt no cosmic shudder when he'd left Seaview and this embarrassed her. As if we, her audience, had expected telepathy. But then, over the next few days, she seemed to miss Sean. Which was strange to me. They'd spent a total of ninety supervised minutes together each week. Her mourning, which was mostly a sullen lack of interest in our lives, felt larger than the loss itself.

A week after Sean's departure, a letter arrived for Maeve. She carried it with her all day and reread it at every moment of repose, including throughout lunch and dinner. We got tired of asking her what it said, she never answered. The next day she had a long meeting with her team. They were supposed to reevaluate her double-probation status. She didn't join us until after dinner. When we asked her how it went, she just said fine.

That night, a full hour after lights-out, Maeve knocked at my door. It wasn't quite a knock; she tapped her fingers against the frame. I got up and tied my robe, a long flannel gift from Syd. They had not been able to set a moratorium on presents, and she had mailed a stream of comforts—plush towels, scented soaps, cashmere socks, and a green-and-black-striped robe. I opened the door a crack and Maeve pushed in.

"Get dressed," she said.

I fumbled for the light, then squinched my eyes.

"We're going out," she said. "Hurry."

She was all dressed up, a tiny vinyl dress and high-heeled shoes. I said, "You're wearing that?"

"What don't you like?"

Maeve waved Sean's letter. She read three long, inarticulate paragraphs about how he couldn't live without her. I realized she'd kept it from us in order to increase our interest in his homely correspondence. With Maeve, reticence was always a prelude to display: why did I forget that? In the last paragraph Sean mentioned a local bar, the Depot. It was a mile from Seaview. He said he went there every night.

"So much for sobriety," I said.

"He just drinks ginger ale."

"Oh," I said.

"There you go again." Maeve crossed to my chest of drawers. "That 'oh' business." She pulled out half my tops and threw them on the bed. "Don't you own anything cute?"

I started refolding the discarded clothes. I have a particular way of folding; no one else ever does it right. I said, "And how are we supposed to get to there?"

"Sean's giving us a ride."

I said, "You've forgotten they lock the doors at night?"

She held up three keys.

"Where'd you get those?"

"Sean's brother is a security systems specialist."

"A what?"

"A locksmith. They mailed three different master keys."

"They? So this is a double date?"

"For fuck's sake, Alice, do me a favor, will you? Can you do me a goddamn favor? I've done enough for you."

"So I entertain the deadbeat brother while you spend the evening in the men's john screwing Sean, is that it?"

"Alice, I would never do that."

"Of course you would! You did it here, for crying out loud!"

"Okay. All right. I would, but I won't. I promise. Look, we'll play pool. I'm a great pool player. We'll play the girls against the boys. Two games and we'll go home. No, three. Three games, tops. For Christ's sake, I'll hold your hand the whole night if you want. They love that anyway."

"Maeve!"

"Alice, please." She actually got down on her knees. It was no easy feat in that tight little dress; she had to hold the corner of the bed and lower herself one leg at a time.

I said, "Don't patronize me."

She said, "Please come."

I said, "Don't treat me the way you treat them. Get up."

"I'm afraid to go alone."

"Get up!"

"I need to go so bad."

"You're not afraid of anything."

"Of course I am."

"Like what?"

"Like, I don't know. How would you put it? Like not being seen," she said.

"You're seen already! You're seen! Everyone sees you. My God, who doesn't see you?"

"The shrinks, for one."

"Please. Who do they see?"

"Okay then, you. You don't see me."

"Of course I see you. I see you on your knees in front of me right now. Please get up."

"If you really saw me, you'd see how bad I need to do this."

"Are you that stuck on Sean?"

"No."

"What then?"

She got off the floor. It was hardly graceful. Her ankles wobbled in the shoes. "I just can't stay in this miserable shithole another minute."

"Why?"

"I just can't."

"But why? All of a sudden?"

"Gwen."

I quieted down. I stared at my two-sizes-too-big chinos. We didn't say anything for a while.

Then, all matter-of-fact, she said, "Have you noticed the irony, us calling the counselors here shrinks? I mean I know everybody says that now: *shrink* means therapist, *shrinking* means therapy. But it's their job here, you know. They're actually supposed to *shrink* us."

"Not me."

"Yes you."

"How's that?"

"Your ego."

I blinked. I couldn't believe she'd said that.

She put both hands on her hips. "You anorexics. You're so famous to yourselves."

Thirty-three

The parking lot was enormous, a sea of gray with hundreds of conscientious yellow stripes. Tall markers announced separate parking sections, R through Z. We must have been in the back of the lot. It was empty except for three gigantic Dumpsters, which sat openmouthed in the farthest corner, each one a different primary color. Maeve said her favorite was the red. She made us pick one, the way kids do, as if the choosing would make them ours. I took blue. Sean was left with yellow. He said the Dumpsters had been color-coded for different kinds of medical waste. He said he had liked to climb up on his bureau to watch from the small square window in his room as the orderlies rolled out the various bags of noxious trash. I was surprised he knew the word *noxious*, until I remembered he was a fireman.

It was raining out. Fat, splashy drops that we could hear land. We hadn't worn coats. We were traveling light. Sean's brother Pat had parked behind the Dumpsters—they were afraid of being spotted—and we had to slosh through the rain. Maeve could hardly take a regular step in her shoes. Sean put his satin Red Sox jacket over her shoulders and an arm around her waist. Maeve took my hand. I was shivering. We walked awkwardly, a threesome in our own five-legged race.

Maeve had not found anything cute in my entire wardrobe. She was on the verge of going back for one of her own blouses when Sean arrived. He tossed a piece of gravel against my second-story window, which was probably two-foot square. Maeve gave me ten fingers to hoist me up to the double pane of glass; I waved. By the time we'd crept down the stairs to the emergency exit next to the gym, I realized the extent to which she'd counted on my acquiescence: she'd given Sean directions to my window instead of hers.

The big steel door was alarmed, meaning it wasn't locked and you could push it open, but an alarm would sound, bringing not only doctors and nurses, but the police and fire departments as well. The second of the master keys worked. Sean was waiting when we opened the heavy door. He said proudly that Pat had declared the security system "violable." I told myself at least they knew big words. Sean put a piece of electrical tape over the latch so we could get back in.

The brother was a dopey-looking version of Sean. Same red face and hair, same Clark Kent appeal, only squishy instead of robust. His body was thicker and softer. His face was open. Unlike his brother, Pat had no cocaine-edge. He opened the passenger door to their pickup truck. It was an old Chevrolet with a wide, patched front seat instead of buckets. The skinny stick shift jiggled on the metal floor, and tufts of yellowed stuffing strained like overgrowth through holes in the upholstery. The front seat was not quite big enough to accommodate us four comfortably, but we all climbed in, Pat in the driver's seat, his huge, lethargic hand a paw on the ball of the shift, me next, squeezed into the small-est space possible, then, predictably, Maeve on Sean's lap. For the whole of the ride, I concentrated on keeping my knees from touching the stick shift, while Pat talked apolo-getically and without pause about the shabbiness of the truck, his voice rising over the shaking metal. I could feel the four of us pretending to ignore Maeve's careful adjustments on Sean's lap; not that we could see his erection, but still, we knew it was there. We sensed its presence in the cab of the truck, almost like another person whom we tried to make room for, an additional listener to Pat's contrite voice.

The Depot was set diagonally across from the Grey-hound bus terminal, a long flat building painted to look like a railroad car. A real switch light, from a real railroad, stood at the entrance. Several big American cars and other, newer pickup trucks were parked out front.

Pat went ahead to grab the door. Sean held his coat above us like a giant umbrella. I touched Maeve's elbow. "Three games, right, and then we go home?"

"Relax," she said, pulling down her dress, which had crawled up an inch during the ride. "And don't call it home."

"They'll kick us out," I whispered.

"I'm already three-quarters gone."

"They'll kick *me* out."

She stopped and turned to look at me full face. Her eyes had lost their green again, the pupils flat and big as quarters.

"Not you. They're too intent on curing you, Alice. Look how much they've already fattened you up."

It was the first time she was intentionally cruel to me.

Sean herded us with gentle elbow pokes. Once we were inside, the initial barroom din—the tap and crack of pool, jukebox music, men's voices, the crashing rain of beer bottles—paused. Pat and Sean moved like football tackles, Pat first, steering us through the smoke and denim bodies, Sean bringing up the rear. We began a wave of turning heads and quieted conversation; the only other women in the bar looked spent at thirty. There were three well-kept pool tables in the back, polished wood with bright green felt.

We found some empty chairs, and the boys dropped their coats to claim them. Maeve sent Pat to the bar for drinks (a Tom Collins for her, a Shirley Temple for me), Sean to commandeer a pool table. There was a protocol for joining in, and besides that, a long line. Maeve insisted that the men waiting to play would relent; they did. Sean paid them. While he was making the final arrangements, Maeve began a practice round, grabbing the first stick offered. It took her only seconds to aim and hit the balls. They cracked like gunfire, like those sulfur-smelling caps from childhood.

I said, "You weren't kidding you're a terrific pool player."

She smiled and twisted the tip of her cue into one of the little blue pots of chalk that reminded me of eye shadow. "It's a living," she said. She moved confidently between shots, her eyes focused on the bright hard balls, imagining their trajectories. She even banked one: the white ball bumped one, two, three felt walls before grazing a blue ball and easing it into a pocket. There was something different about the way she moved.

I said, "You don't play pool for a living?" I laughed nervously. Ha. Ha.

She said, "No."

We both smiled. Ha. Ha. I laughed again.

"But remember this, Alice. When men hustle pool, they usually lose the first few games, but women who hustle have to win straight out. Or they won't be taken seriously and they'll never get a game."

I felt very, very cold.

She retrieved a can of talcum powder from under the table and shook it on the stick. She powdered her hands. There was a looseness in her wrists and fingers.

What I didn't understand was how she became so suddenly, so utterly strange. "Can I ask you something?"

"Sure."

"You're not a librarian, are you?"

She shook her head.

The balls hurried into their pockets, silent after the initial tap, stealthy on the felt. She missed twice.

When the table was empty except for the white ball, I said, "Why'd you say you were a librarian?"

"Because I wanted you to like me. People like what they know."

"Does anyone else at Seaview know you're not a librarian?"

"Just Louise."

"Does Louise know everything?"

"More than most."

"Why Louise?"

Maeve shrugged. "She has low expectations."

Pat brought the drinks, all four in his left hand. There were two Shirley Temples, one for me, one for Sean, each topped with a slice of orange and a cherry. "We haven't been formally introduced," he said. He held out his massive right hand. "Pat. Donovan."

"Alice. Alice Forrester."

And I said to myself right then, This is a nice, nice man. But I knew it didn't matter. We were out of our league. Or I was. AWOL from Seaview. Syd would kill me for this—the money she'd spent. Stranded in a bar. Maeve in that ridiculous dress. Entirely dependent on the good intentions of two men who, no matter how nice, must have been hoping for some reimbursement. One (maybe both of them, what did I know, really?) a drug addict. And Maeve, unrecognizable in her greed. I thought of all the things I'd so carefully given up: hunger, need, dependence of any kind. How had she duped me, too? How had she brought me here, so far away from safety? I felt totally alone. But not the alone of being walled-up inside myself. The alone of being wide-open, defenseless. More than anything in the world I wanted to see a familiar face. And then, out of nowhere, I did.

I felt the snap of relief inside my chest. A rush of lightness. I dropped Pat's hand and took a half-step toward the person I knew. Who was it? A man. The face didn't immediately register. An acquaintance from college? It took a second. He was coming closer. It was Dr. Paul.

Everything in the universe shrank.

"Hello, Miss Forrester," he said. "Hello, Miss Sullivan. What a pleasant, pleasant surprise."

Thirty-four

Unbelievably, he joined us. He said he'd love to play pool. He shook Sean's hand, asked about his job. He said, "I hope your reentry is going well." We were terrified. He smiled at Maeve and me. He bowed. "At your service, ladies." This was the way he let it be known: he could ruin each of us, if he wanted to. "I'm not much of a pool player," he confessed. "Who'll be my coach?" He looked innocently from face to face.

But he didn't want to ruin us. He wanted something else. Of course we knew what it was.

Maeve said, "I'll be your coach, sure."

Sean took Pat to the bar to explain the situation. I watched the two of them argue, unable to hear the words, but able to make sense of the angry gesticulations. Pat slammed his drink on the table. Sean made a shooing gesture, his hands waving in front of him, accidentally feminine, like a girl dancing the hula. Finally Pat left, cursing his brother, bumping against bystanders as he made his way out the Depot door.

Maeve had started Paul's lesson with the stick and chalk. She got out the talcum powder. She knew instinctively about power. How to treat it. How to gain access. It was like watching a spotlight move suddenly from a secondary player to the star, who has just wandered in, unexpected, from offstage. In a weird way, she didn't seem to mind.

Dr. Paul was an earnest student, standing close to catch every word. Maeve bent his thick fingers into a grip for the tip of the stick. I saw the delight on his face as she held the fat end of the cue and threaded it through. Sean and I watched numbly. So much had changed so quickly. Maeve was now Dr. Paul's date. I belonged to Sean. His fear had eclipsed his anger, but not his desire, which had become like a blister, like an abscessed pain in his thigh. He moved stiff-legged around the pool table.

Dr. Paul's lesson took a while. By the time he was ready to play, he was comfortable touching her—the fleshy upper arms, the flat, freckled wrists. Once he put his hand on her hip.

As Maeve had promised, we played the boys against the girls. Eight ball. She was better than all three of us put together.

Our team won the first game quickly. Maeve didn't miss until her fifth shot, after which we each had a turn. Sean sank two balls, Paul and I sank none. When Maeve's turn came back around, she sank the rest.

The men in the bar noticed. A few jeered at Sean while we played. A group of spectators formed around our pool table, and I could hear people taking bets.

We won the second game almost as quickly as the first. Dr. Paul sank two balls but blew the third. I lined up the cue stick and missed the ball entirely, the stick seeming to jump out of my hands. Sean came over to demonstrate proper form. He wrapped his bulky arms around mine. Dr. Paul smiled and rested his hand on the small of Maeve's back, pleased that the distribution of property had come out right. He whispered in her ear.

Sean's lesson was effective, if temporary; I sank my shot. Maeve clapped. Sean made an effort at good humor; he slapped me on the back. I sputtered and coughed. The next ball I hit skittered across the table and pocketed one of theirs. Sean sank three in a row; they had six out of seven. Maeve sank each of our remaining balls, plus the black one, the eight, all in a single turn. Several men cheered.

Someone in the crowd said, "She's got really soft hands."

Dr. Paul conceded defeat, his arms open, his smile generous. I remembered Maeve's first day, when I went downstairs and found her with him. He had offered the same false humility.

Maeve handed him her stick, and said, "We're going to freshen up. How about another drink when we get back?"

The bathroom was small and filthy, the standard women's john in bars with mostly male patrons. Maeve took me with her into the single dilapidated stall and made me stand against the wooden door, which had no lock. She put down the toilet seat cover and sat, her hands in her lap. The bathroom stank. She said, "Are you okay?"

"I guess. My head's spinning."

"Mine too."

"You've certainly got your hands full," I said.

"And I'm not doing too badly, if I do say so myself."

"You sound awfully proud."

"Maybe I am."

"You can't be enjoying this."

Maeve folded her arms across her chest. "I had a boyfriend once who was a high school football coach. He told me that the secret of a successful football team is the ability to adapt to sudden change. That's all this is, Alice. I'm adapting to sudden change."

"I want to go home."

She stood up in the cramped stall. "It's not home!" She shouted, "Don't call it home."

I could feel the panic start. Gert said addiction took many forms. Could this be one? This love of frenzy? I said, "I want to leave. I don't—I can't get kicked out."

She sat back down. "I don't know why you're in such a rush to get to Seaview. Believe me, it'll still be there. Besides, we're just getting started."

"What's that supposed to mean?"

She opened her folded palms. A small glass vial rested in the fleshy cup. It was dark brown, not quite opaque.

"Is that what I think it is?"

"None other."

I'd never done cocaine. Or any drug. What with all my starving, it seemed an overstatement. "I thought you said Sean was clean."

She held the vial up to the dingy bathroom light. "He is. This is courtesy of the good doctor."

"I don't believe you."

"He wants to assure our nice time."

"Meaning—"

"He wants to fuck me."

"Jesus."

"Relax, Alice. Don't be such a scaredy cat. Men do this. Especially shrimpy ones. It's been going on for centuries, for Christ's sake. Where have you been? And for as long as men have been giving women cocaine so that women will fuck them, women have been doing their cocaine and not fucking them. Relax. I can handle this. Believe me, I've handled worse. This little troll of a man is nothing."

Maeve unscrewed the cap. There was a thin piece of metal attached to it. She used the silver stick-spoon to stir the powder. She looked like she was cooking miniature food. I pictured the tiny cake that would come of this. She balanced a pile of cocaine on the rounded end of the spoon. She brought it up to her right nostril, rested a moment, and sniffed. The white stuff disappeared. It seemed a shock. She squeezed her left eye shut and pinched both nostrils. She sniffed at the air repeatedly, the way you sniff a runny nose. It was the first wholly graceless thing I'd seen her do. She capped the vial. "Your turn." She offered it to me.

I didn't move.

Maeve said, "What's the matter?"

I shrugged.

"Don't tell me you haven't done this before?"

I shook my head.

"Alice, what *have* you been doing for the last ten years?"

"Counting calories," I said. "Really, it's been more or less full-time."

She laughed. For a few seconds, I glimpsed the Maeve I knew. She smiled, stood up, and started stirring again. She said, "I want you to exhale slowly through your nose. When your breath is completely out, hold it, and I'll put the spoon under one nostril. Then inhale really sharply. It's sort of a snort, like they say. Cover the other nostril with your thumb." It was a teacherly voice. She could have been showing me diamond cutting, she took that much care.

I did exactly what Maeve said, exhaling and covering one nostril, but when she approached my nose, I panicked and inhaled, then reversed directions. The cocaine blew onto Maeve's hair and dress.

"Shit," she said. She looked down. She licked her fingers and tried to wipe the cocaine off her dress. It slid down the vinyl onto the floor. She picked up her head. "Come here," she said.

"What?" There wasn't anywhere to go. Maeve was right in front of me.

"Come here."

I took a half step forward and immediately stepped on her toe. "See," I said.

She dug a small pile onto her spoon, then capped the vial. She licked a finger and touched it to the whiteness. The cocaine stuck. "Open your mouth," she said.

Before I could protest, Maeve reached one arm around my neck and slipped the wetted finger inside my mouth. She rubbed the cocaine along my top gum. It was bitter, metallic, the taste of traveled pennies. She opened the vial again; this was awkward, my head was tucked against her shoulder. I didn't move. She ground in another pile, tracing a line along the tops of my teeth. My gums began to go numb, like after novocaine. I looked up. Maeve had a funny expression on her face; a mixture of satisfaction and pain. She leaned her face quite close to mine. At first I thought she was inspecting her work, looking for white powder traces. But instead of examining my mouth, she kissed it.

A real kiss: full-lipped, with tongue, teeth, and whiskey-flavored spit. Her tongue was bigger than I'd thought possible. I felt it fill my mouth—its tip, veiny bottom and sides. The taste-bud roughened top. She ran it along my teeth, across the numbing gums.

She pulled back a moment and looked at me. Her eyes were out of focus and her upper lip had curled, just the littlest bit, into a sneer. For a second, I thought, Does she know who I am? She kissed me again. This time I couldn't feel any particular part of my mouth, just her inside me. She jammed her tongue in and out, ramming our teeth. It felt funny. I wanted her to stop. Her hand reached around to the back of my head and pulled my hair. "Do you know what I'm doing?" she said.

I shook my head, but she pulled my hair tighter and I had to stop.

"I'm fucking your mouth," she said.

It felt like the back of my head came off. I closed my eyes and she did it some more.

Thirty-five

Maeve announced that we would have to go after the third game. Dr. Paul seemed to agree. He looked at his Cartier watch. It was understood that he, not Sean, would be driving us back. Only Sean was despondent. For the first time that evening, I could breathe. Maybe this wouldn't end so badly. Maybe Sister Geraldine was wrong: maybe some sins, like stupidity, went unpunished. While Dr. Paul was figuring out which balls to aim at, stripes or solids, Maeve smiled at Sean. His longing was acute. Maeve missed her first shot intentionally. So did Sean. Dr. Paul and I played with determination—we both wanted to go—but desire didn't improve our games. Dr. Paul knocked the white ball clear off the table; it made a clacking noise on the wood-planked floor. I sank only two balls after several turns.

The cocaine had not seemed to affect me much, other than assuring my silence. My lips and tongue and gums were rubber. Not that I had anything to say. And Maeve seemed the same. She was not louder or more exuberant. What was cocaine for, I thought, if we were left unchanged? The high-pitched whine behind my ears? The way my eyelids yawned but refused to close? There were pieces of lint on the green felt table that I hadn't noticed before. Was that what all the excitement was about? This visual acuity? Perhaps I hadn't done enough. I could understand how people wanted more. I watched Maeve.

It had been a surprise to leave the ladies' john and have no one see. Perhaps this was the ironic rush of doing

cocaine: you could see what nobody else could. There was
not a single comment about our flushed faces, Maeve's brim-
ming eyes. I was worried when we finally stumbled out,
what exactly would they be able to tell? But the men seemed
oblivious to what we had done.

And what had we done?

Maeve had kissed me.

No. We had kissed.

The truth was, I had kissed her back. My tongue had
gone for hers.

It had not even been nice, the way kissing Ronald in
high school had been. It had been urgent, insistent, extreme.
It felt more necessary than good. Like a bodily function.

I had always thought that after something like this, it
would be—one would be—immediately identifiable. When I
walked out of the bathroom door, the word *lezzy* lay between
the flat of my tongue and the base of my lower front teeth,
the place the *l* would start were I to say it. I was afraid the
word would fall out in response to some innocuous question: "Have you ever played pool before?"

"Lezzy," I would say.

Not *lesbian* or *homosexual*.

"Another Shirley Temple?"

"Lezzy." It would slip out again.

The seventh-grade word. Not the words I had
learned in college about sexual preference and alternative
lifestyles and wimmin loving wimmin. Not the adult words.

Of all the things I'd ever imagined for myself, I'd
never pictured this. But then it occurred to me. I did not love
women. I loved Maeve.

Was there a word for that?

I didn't think so.

Which made it easier.

Perhaps it was a small distinction. I didn't care.

I held on to it.

Maeve finally won. I sighed, relieved. We would be
going home.

"That's it?"

"That's it." Maeve nodded. She handed Paul her stick. "We have to be going now."

I gave him mine. He was relieved too. He was tired of pool. He wanted what came next. He walked the three pool cues to the nearest rack-lined wall. When Paul reached up to put them in place, Sean grabbed Maeve by the waist and pulled her through the crowd. They were leaving. Their heads bobbed above a field of work shirts. My heart leapt frantically inside my chest, and I thought, I'm going to die. They were almost at the door. I put my hand to my mouth. I burped up cherry-sweetened ginger ale, those bitter pennies. I felt a pain in my chest. I wouldn't just die; Dr. Paul would kill me.

But they didn't leave. They stopped to the left of the Depot door. Something was there. I craned my neck. The jukebox. Maeve and Sean bowed over the selection of songs. I pushed my way forward. I had to see. Sean dropped quarters down the slot. Maeve ran her hand along the glass front, then punched in several numbers. The evening's music had all sounded like one song, the screech of glass on metal.

There was no dance floor to speak of, just enough room to stand and pick songs. She'd found a sweet, old Motown tune, probably the only one on the box. Sean wrapped both arms around her, his fingers splayed against her ribs. They rocked in place. You could hardly call it dancing. I found them difficult to watch. Not Dr. Paul. He'd made it through the crowd and now stood next to me, hands on hips, eyes riveted. He shifted his weight from one foot to the next. I didn't want to look at him.

Maeve danced with her eyes closed and her mouth partially open. Did jealousy feel like disgust? Is that what this was? I could feel Dr. Paul's fury at my side. We hated each other. Leftovers both.

When the song ended, Maeve let go of Sean. Dr. Paul stepped up. Somehow Maeve made the men shake hands, like good-natured uncles sharing the bride. Dr. Paul moved her toward the door. I trailed after, looking back, over my shoulder, for Sean. I wasn't an expert in these things, but I thought I saw despair.

The air outside felt good, refreshing. It was colder. The rain had turned to April snow drops. Not real flakes, they landed wet like rain. I had started counting to myself: how long until we were safe in Seaview beds? I was up to thirty-nine. *Forty. Forty-one. Forty-two.* Maeve hummed softly.

Dr. Paul's car was parked behind the Depot so we hadn't seen it coming in. We would have taken note. It was baby blue, half as big and half as vulgar as a Corvette, but with the same dip and roll of the hood. Maeve knew the name of the car, and she said it out loud, appreciatively, but it was too late. Dr. Paul unlocked her door and held it open until I'd climbed in the back and Maeve had seated herself. She reached across and unlocked his. Once inside, he did not say anything but motioned to indicate her seat belt. There was a sour smell in the car. I thought he was sweating, but maybe it was just the rain-dampness of our clothes. From where I sat, his crown was lustrous.

I could see Dr. Paul's anger and disappointment in every gesture. His meaty hand clutched and released the stick shift, clutched and released in a rhythmic way that made me lonesome for Sean and Pat's lumpy truck. Maeve pretended not to notice anything wrong. She rolled down the window and stuck out her head. The night sky was yellowish from the snow. She took great gulps of air and let the snow splash her face. Paul warmed the engine. I watched his hands move from the steering wheel to the stick shift. I wondered how many times a day he washed them. Even underneath the fingernails was a shiny white. He told Maeve to roll up the window. I counted. *Eighty-seven. Eighty-eight. Eighty-nine. Ninety.* We were on our way.

He drove very fast. The car accelerated with ease. He never let go of the stick and went up to the highest gear after each stop. It would have been less work to drive in a lower gear. These were suburban streets, and it was snowing, after all. But he shifted again and again and again. You could tell he really wanted to.

We parked by the same emergency exit. When Maeve opened the car door to get out, Dr. Paul grabbed her. "Wait," he said. "I want to talk." He held her left wrist tightly.

Maeve sat back, the door ajar. The wet snow poured in. "So talk," she said.

"Alone."

Maeve sighed. "Alice," she said. She sounded tired. "Would you give Paul and I a moment?"

I said, "Maeve—"

"It'll just take a moment, I'm sure. Isn't that right, Paul?"

He glared at her. "Two minutes tops," he said.

I said, "I don't think it's a good idea." *Three hundred seventeen. Three hundred eighteen.*

Maeve wrenched free from Dr. Paul's grip. She turned around in her seat. "Get out of the car," she said to me. "Give us a minute."

I shook my head.

"The sooner you get out, the sooner we get back inside."

"I don't like it."

"The ability to adapt to sudden change," she whispered.

I started to cry.

She pulled her seat forward for me to climb out.

I caught a chill the moment I stepped onto the pavement. The snow fell in soggy clumps, as if two and three flakes were piggybacking on the way down. Dr. Paul reached across Maeve and pulled the door shut after me. I heard him lock it. *Three hundred thirty-two. Three hundred thirty-three.* He put the car in gear and sped away. I stopped counting.

It looked like a Matchbox car as it looped the parking

lot, a pretty sky blue Matchbox, as it drove behind the Dumpsters, first past Maeve's favorite, the red, then past mine, a darker blue than the car. He stopped behind the Dumpster that had been assigned to Sean in Maeve's silly game. Dr. Paul would have chosen another if he'd known. It was canary yellow, vibrant, the color Gwen had used to make her hair in art therapy. The three Dumpsters were staggered, each one a few feet behind the other; the yellow was the farthest. Maeve's was the closest, bright and full of warning. Red was for infectious waste, Sean had said.

They seemed a half a mile away.

I hadn't run in years, and it felt terrible. The bones in my legs flopped against skin, as if they were moving not in unison, but in opposite directions. My muscles wavered, gelatinous, loose. Had they come away from the bone? My knees and ankles cracked. I had to stop midway to catch my breath. Pain raged at my side; my stomach was in my throat. I ran-walked, ran-walked. My loafers pinched my toes.

"Shit," I said. "Shit, shit, shit."

Up close, the Dumpsters were twice as tall as me. Monster mouths from some high-tech action movie. When I got to Paul's little blue car, I was thoroughly wet. Exhaust steamed in puffy white clouds behind the car. The windows fogged. I threw up. Something I hadn't done in years. Maraschino-flavored ginger ale and orange pulp. The taste of pennies lingered. I bent over, my hands on my knees, and threw up some more. Just bile. It landed on the ground between my feet. It splattered my shoes.

For the first time in my life I wanted to be huge. Absolutely huge. As big as one of the Dumpsters, as big as three Seans stacked on top of each other. I wanted to be big enough to pick up the car and hurl it across the parking lot. I wanted to sit on Paul and crush him with my weight. I wanted to hear his chest explode.

I wiped my mouth on my shirtsleeve and made my way to the car. I couldn't see inside. I made a fist and pounded on Maeve's window until my knuckles started to bleed. I ran to the driver's side and pounded with the heel of my palm. There was no strength anywhere in my body. How had I let that happen? How come I had never pictured needing to be strong? If not for me, at least for someone else? I took a loafer off and, standing on one foot, smashed the shoe against Paul's window. I thought I heard a sound from inside. I put my shoe over my sopping sock and hoisted myself up, head and torso first, red hands gripping the wipers for leverage, onto the hood. It was too slippery to stand. I lay across the windshield, my face against the glass. Maybe I could shame him into stopping. There was a loud, unmistakable noise from inside the car. I thought I might throw up again. A minute passed. The passenger door opened and Maeve's feet, then legs, slid out. She bent forward to put on her shoes. When she stood, her thighs shaking, she brushed off her knees. She shut the car door without looking back. I climbed off the hood.

She looked surprised to see me, surprised by the Dumpsters, surprised by the cold air. The snowflakes startled her. Her whole appearance, but especially her face, looked shrunken. She had something in her hand. She looked at it quizzically. I couldn't see what it was through the clumpy snow. She teetered on her shoes. The car backed up. Dr. Paul was in a hurry. He drove away.

I started to sob out loud. Maeve opened her mouth and jammed her fingers down her throat. She didn't even have to bend. She arched her body slightly; Tom Collinses poured out of her. For a second she looked like a real fountain. Like the statue in Pygmalion turning back into stone. But then she looked like how she really was: cold, wet, ruined. She threw up a second time, then a third. I wailed in the snowy rain.

When she finished puking, Maeve walked over to me. I was crying so hard I couldn't catch my breath. My heart was pounding. My temples ached. She showed me what was in her hands: two perfect rows of teeth. She popped them back in her mouth and smiled. Her beautiful model's teeth so free of bulimic moss had been fake all along. She cupped her hands around my mouth. Her fingers smelled of puke, but I caught my breath in the small, hot space she made with her hands. She put one arm around my waist and pulled me toward the hospital.

Thirty-six

O
ur footsteps echoed in the empty stairwell. Maeve made us take off our shoes.

"What happened?" I leaned against her, removed one loafer. "I thought you said you could handle things?"

"They haven't caught us yet, have they?"

I snorted. It felt good to snort at Maeve. "You know that's not what I mean."

"So he had more resources than I thought."

"You said you'd handled worse." I hated her for being wrong.

"He said he'd tell on us. On Sean. If I didn't cooperate. He has records. He could contact Sean's job."

"So you, you—" I started crying again.

"For Christ's sake, Alice. I did it half as much for you as I did for myself."

"You shouldn't have. You shouldn't have done that for me. I'd rather we get kicked out."

"Well, thanks. Thanks for telling me. Now." She spat the words. "After. It was all you could talk about at the Depot. Not getting kicked out. Well, now you're *home*."

Maeve tucked my loafers and her pumps under one arm. I couldn't seem to stop crying. She steered me to the first-floor shower, the one attached to the gym. She said we'd be less likely to be discovered; since no one slept on the first floor, no nurses were assigned there. One of the master keys fit the door to the four interconnecting gym rooms. She sat me on the bench nearest the showers in the locker room.

Her dress came off, with difficulty, straight over her head. There was nothing underneath. She tiptoed naked, arms across her chest for warmth, to turn on showers. She adjusted their temperatures. She came back for me, but I was still crying.

"Enough," she said.

I sniveled. "Everything hurts."

"When did you get hurt?"

"From running."

"You ran?"

I nodded. "To the car. I couldn't save you."

She smiled. "I wasn't expecting you to."

"I was."

"Oh, Alice."

She undressed me. Our clothes made a soggy pile. I heard the shower hiss. Steam licked and climbed the tile walls. Maeve led me by the hand.

The water was hard at first, prickly. It stung my skin and made me wince. Maeve adjusted the showerheads until the water fell in soft swollen drops that didn't hurt. She walked back and forth between the sprays of the two separate showerheads.

"I wish we had a real sauna," she said.

I stood limply by the first spray, not crying, listening and watching her move. Steam curled at the ceiling.

"We deserve one after the night we've had."

I'd never seen her completely naked, just whatever part she'd wanted to show. She weighed maybe fifty pounds more than I—half my body weight. She had long legs and a long fleshy middle. Lines like wrinkles stretched across her abdomen. When she bent to retrieve the soap, the lines folded into rolls of fat. I counted three. They disappeared when she stood.

"Soap?" She offered me the bar.

I shook my head. I didn't have the heart for getting clean.

"Come on." She walked over to me. Everything

shimmied: breasts, belly, thigh. I could see the cords of her stomach muscles.

She was not what I expected. She was not precise.

She forced my head directly under the stream of water. It closed out every other sound. I rested. She soaped me: armpits, bum, between my legs. All the smelly parts. The soap washed away the instant she sudsed.

When I stepped out of the stream, she pointed at my pubic hair. "Don't you ever cut this stuff?"

I looked down. Black ringlets coiled against my thigh. Maeve's hair was cut in a flat, neat triangle. I could see two pink lips. My hair was wooly by comparison. It hadn't occurred to me to trim this. I felt a flash of heat across my skin.

"You're gonna need one of Gwen's French braids pretty soon."

Maeve held on to the backs of my thighs as she crouched and soaped each leg. She rubbed in circles around my knees. She lifted both feet and washed between my toes. She massaged the soles with the knuckles of her fisted hand.

When she was finished with me, she stood on her toes beneath one of the showerheads. Stretching out as tall as possible, she tipped her mouth toward the water and caught the hard shower rain. She rinsed and spat three times.

We didn't have towels. We stood in front of the paper towel dispenser and cranked the lever. We were trembling, making puddles on the floor, but we weren't as cold as we'd been. Maeve punched the button on the hand dryer. It warmed her midriff as she dried her hair. The paper towel soaked through and came apart in our hands. We cranked and cranked.

I felt better. Less despairing. Almost refreshed. I said, "You know we have to put those wet clothes on again to go upstairs."

"Shit," said Maeve.

We looked at the pile.

She said, "Maybe we should blow-dry the clothes."

I said, "I'm afraid the heat might melt your dress."

"Fuck you." She laughed. We laughed. The first time since leaving the Depot. It hurt my ribs but felt good, like peeing after holding it a long while.

"We used to do that in swim team," I said.

"Do what?"

"Use the hand dryer on our bodies."

She looked down at her dry stomach. "So you're a good swimmer?"

"Pretty good."

"You can do flip turns?"

"Uh-huh."

"I could never do those."

"They're tricky."

"Let's see." She threw a clump of sodden paper towels in the wastebasket and stepped away from the dryer. "Let's go for a swim."

I should have put my foot down then. I should have said, Give it a rest. Let's don't push our luck. A person might think, after the night we'd had, that I wouldn't continue to follow her. But I did. Maeve took too much effort to resist. And she'd been so careful in the shower. She'd touched every part of my skin. I followed her across the length of the locker room to the pool. On the other side of the Plexiglas wall sat the square black lake, its surface still.

"Look at how flat it is," I whispered. "They must shut the filters off at night."

She pushed open the door. The room was warm, the air a mix of chlorine and mildew. Maeve searched the walls for a light. Her hands ran across the tile. She found three switches, tried them all, then left only one, a spot from the ceiling that fell into the middle of the pool. The corners and sides stayed dark.

"Not great lighting for demonstrating flip turns," I said.

She sat on the pool's edge, then lowered herself down. She crouched until the water surrounded her breasts.

I wondered if a person could actually feel her adrenal glands working.

"Come on," Maeve said. "It's warm."

I wanted to dive. The water was shallow, five feet at its deepest. A racing dive then, to skim the surface. I wanted to show Maeve something I could do.

I shot out, over the water, my body flat like an eel. At the last moment, I arched faintly and dipped, fingers first, into the black-green pool. I made little noise, less splash.

Maeve was smiling when I came up. "Bravo!"

The water was dark green in the center of the pool, where the light shone down, then murky, then black at the edges. I swam two laps underwater. Maeve's legs turned to face me as I groped past. I'd never swum naked before. It felt like losing a layer of skin. I watched my own pubic hair bunch and sway.

"I used to be able to stay under longer," I said when I came up. "Syd and I stayed down for so long at the beach, Dad and Alex would come running into the water."

Maeve said, "You used to swim together a lot, you and your mother?"

I nodded. It occurred to me that I knew almost nothing about Maeve. I wondered how she had been able to be the center of attention for so long, yet reveal so little of herself. I said, "What about your mother?"

"My mother?"

"Yes, what's she like?"

"She's not a swimmer, that's for sure."

"Well, what then? What does she do?"

"Do? She doesn't do anything. She's just a mother."

I didn't know what that meant. I couldn't picture Maeve's mother being domestic. "She doesn't work, then?"

"She works." Maeve waved a hand in the air as if to close the subject. "Come on, let's see those fancy turns."

I did flip turns and then some of the easier synchronized moves Syd had taught me, the Eiffel Tower, the clamshell, a flying camel into a sailor's spin. Maeve was pleased. I taught her how to do a simple kick turn, then spotted her for underwater somersaults. She kept panicking and putting one leg out to feel the floor. It was hard to teach flip turns in shallow water.

Maeve swallowed some pool and came up coughing. I said, "Let's rest." I watched her catch her breath. Her chest heaved, the nipples tipped just under. Her thick hair was wrapped round her throat. She pulled it back behind her ears, arranged it in one big chunk. I could tell she was relaxed again. She dove under and swam toward me. She seemed more solid at the bottom of the pool, less jiggly. She gripped my ankles and pulled herself through the opening between my legs.

When she surfaced, I blurted out: "Do you have brothers and sisters?"

Maeve moved the hair off her face. "What is it, Alice?"

"I just . . . I know so little about you. It seems unfair."

"Unfair to who?"

"Both of us."

She thought about that. "You want to know was I abandoned by my mother or abused by my father or beaten up by my brothers? You want to know what happened to make me this way?"

"I just want to know about you. You know about me."

"What I object to in all this therapy crap is the idea that saying it out loud is somehow going to make the horrible details of your life less horrible. That all this fucking sharing brings catharsis. And that, for example, if you know my father left my mother when I was two and a half and fucked every woman he could get his hands on in our hometown for years after and my older brothers locked him in a closet once to keep him from banging on me and he broke one of their arms when he got out, you will be able, first of all, to understand why I do what I do and, second of all, you will be able to explain it to me. As if I couldn't."

"Is that true?"

"For fuck's sake, Alice. Let's just swim."

I dove down and started swimming the same way she had, back and forth between her legs. My mind was racing with the information she'd given me. I tried to picture her parents. On the floor of the pool, I snaked a figure eight, swimming sideways around each leg. When I was halfway through my second pass, Maeve kicked me. I looked up. Her face wavered, distorted by the water but clearly changed. Something was wrong. The pool got suddenly bright. I surfaced. All the lights were on. The night nurse was there.

I didn't have time to feel ashamed. The two of us swimming naked. Me between Maeve's legs. The night nurse was businesslike, not angry. She brought us towels, two apiece. She woke no one escorting us to our rooms. She told us we should go to meditation in the morning and then expect to meet with our teams. They would have things to say.

After she left us, each in our separate rooms, Maeve knocked at my door.

I was afraid to open it but afraid to keep her out. I said through the crack, "Will you stop. You're going to get us killed. Right after they kick us out, they'll strangle us."

She pushed her way in. "I can't sleep alone tonight." She climbed into my single bed. And we slept.

Thirty-seven

———

I woke up terrified. It was dark and I couldn't tell whether it was hours or minutes before dawn. Maeve slept hard, on her belly, one arm over the side of the bed, her knuckles grazing the floor. Her mouth was open, and I could see a string of saliva collecting, bead by bead, at the corner. It was stifling hot. I kicked the covers off my feet and unbuttoned my pajama top. My skin was moist with perspiration. I couldn't remember my dream.

Maeve was wearing a tee shirt and panties, the underwear barely covering the moons of her ass. I put one hand out and touched the freckled skin. It was a word I thought to myself now, since knowing Maeve: *ass*. I used to think *bottom* or *behind* or *bum*. Her flesh was firm and bouncy, as if someone had filled her with water. I cupped my hand around the curve and said the word out loud, "ass," liking the hard sound of the "a." Maeve woke up. I remembered the dream. I was chasing someone.

I moved my hand to the panty, the briefest string bikini, and pulled the cloth upward until it traveled up the crack. There were things I knew about sex. There was that time with Ronald. There were movies. Books I'd read. But I thought this would be different: two women. I wondered whether there were specific lesbian acts. If so, how would I know about them? And if I did, if I did know about them, what did that mean? I whispered into Maeve's waking ear the word *lesbian*.

She didn't turn around. She said, "Are you telling me something or asking me something?"

"I don't know."

"Then let's not worry about it."

"I'm not worried about it. Who's worried?"

I moved my hand down her backside and pulled the panty to one side. I found her opening; she was wet. My fingers slid over the cool fat lips, back and forth. She got wetter. I pushed inside, climbed along the inward slope. I felt the pressure and the pleasure of her resistance and thought, I want this. Maeve curved stiff as an archer's bow, her ass wagging. I pushed in, hard. Then harder. The walls were thick and muscular. She unfolded. With each pass I found more room, like a chamber opening onto another chamber opening onto another. I couldn't do it hard enough. I thought, They call this entering her from behind. If I could have, I would have rammed all of me inside. When she came, she convulsed forward, her whole body shuddering. I wondered if that were good enough. More than anything, I wanted to be good enough. I curled around her, my cheek at her strong shoulder blades, my knees tucked into the crease of hers. Before I fell asleep, I thought, The strangest thing about sex was how much you know when you don't know anything at all.

When I woke, she was on top of me, her tee shirt and panties gone. Her breasts were too big and too floppy to be the breasts in magazines. She had pulled down my pajama bottoms and she sat, her wet sex open—I could smell it, the same soft smell was on my fingers—pressing into mine. Her fleshy stomach glistened. She rubbed against me—tearing pubic hairs—sliding over the ridge—she was wet again, or was it still?—positioning herself over my hip bone—like a dog rutting into mud—she pushed down, her mouth opening, the lip curling into the same ugly sneer as when she'd kissed me. The knobs of my hipbones stood out like elderly bedposts with the thin skin draped across.

She fell forward and ran her heavy breasts across my

stomach. She pressed a nipple into my belly button, and a shock ran through my body. She brought her breasts to my face and just held them there, not moving. I went rigid as a board, my toes pointing to the foot of the bed, my neck arched, my chin tilted at the ceiling. I wanted her to do everything and nothing. I had never known my desire before, and suddenly here it was, so enormous, so pressing, so spectacularly vital and intact, I wanted to hold back and just look at it. But Maeve wouldn't let me. She dragged her nipples slowly across my lips and cheekbones, into the sockets of my eyes. I opened my mouth as wide as it would go, but she kept moving, not letting me taste one, not letting me linger, just an agonizing slow-motion parade of nipple and breast, so I lifted my head from the pillow, my tongue extended. With one firm hand against my forehead, she pushed me down and held me there. She slapped my face with her breasts. I strained toward them until finally she let me suck. And suck. And suck.

Later, when she was inside me, I thought, I won't let go.

In the morning, Gert found us in bed together. She was distraught. She coughed into her hands, not looking as we pulled on clothes, and said, "There's some very bad news."

Thirty-eight

W e thought the bad news would be about us. But
impossibly, we discovered, they did not, would
not, kick us out, not under any circumstances it
seemed, except nonpayment. There would be more team
meetings, more discussion, more group and family therapy.
They were not giving up on us, Gert said.

The bad news was that Gwen was dead.

She had died during the night while we were at the
Depot. While Maeve was shooting pool. While I drank Shirley Temples. A tiny clot of blood, a lump of cells, like curdled
milk, had freed itself from tongue-red tissue and floated up
as Gwen slept, traveling to her lungs. They had lied about
the break: it had not been clean—more of an implosion—
Gwen's hip had disintegrated, like pulverized glass, beneath
her.

Maeve walked down the hall in her too small tee
shirt and panties, got dressed in her room, came back to kiss
me on the mouth, and left the hospital. She left behind her
teal blue American Tourister suitcases, all of her clothes, including the vinyl dress and high-heeled shoes, her impressive collection of purses, two cartons of cigarettes, and me.

That day, I stopped eating.

PART

VI

Thirty-nine

They transferred me back to Medical after two weeks. I was losing weight steadily. They were afraid of another heart attack. I could practically hear them breathe the word *liability*. They put me in the step-down unit, halfway between intensive care and cardiac care. There was a lot of equipment in my room. They were ready for the worst, although I wasn't hooked up to any stationary machines, just a portable heart monitor and the standard IV. I had to wear the heart monitor at all times. It was light, the size of a tape recorder, had a strap like a handbag, and hung loosely under my arm against my chest. I could walk anywhere I wanted in the hospital, they said. But I didn't want to. A nurse got me up to walk twice a day. The physical weakness from not eating was settling in. They were worried about pneumonia. All that time in bed. They made me suck on a hand-held plastic inhaler to expand my lungs. And I got TPN—total parenteral nutrition—a milky intravenous meal of sugar, vitamins, electrolytes, and salt. TPN was a two-bag mix, the first bag twice the size of any other IV, a see-through udder hanging heavily above my head; the second, a small, obnoxiously yellow bag of lipids, dripped alternately with the first. I'd had it last time. It was what Gwen had been on. Syd liked the name. She thought it sounded thorough. They treated me different now, like I was really crazy. I had a psychiatrist instead of a therapist. He wrote prescriptions.

Louise came to visit three days after the transfer. They regretted not having let her visit Gwen. She fidgeted at the foot of my bed, not knowing whether to sit or stand. My room was larger than the one in Psychiatric, the wall above my head a bank of fierce machinery. On one side of the bed there was a square imitation-pine chair with a padded seat and flat armrests; on the other side a miniature bureau with plastic toiletries inside. Louise finally sat at the edge of my bed, lifting a diminished though still substantial haunch gracefully. She looked like a woman who'd gone out for a quart of milk and come back to find her house burned to the ground.

"Please eat something," she said.

I shrugged.

Her weight loss was more and more visible. There were fewer chins; her face was easier to find. Another fifty pounds or so, and she'd be a regular, inoffensive fat person.

She said, "They sent Amy home."

"You're kidding?"

"She actually gained some weight. I don't know why we didn't notice."

"I don't believe it."

"Her agent came to pick her up in a Lincoln Town-car."

"So she really had an agent?"

"Apparently."

"Why is it, Louise, that the craziest people are really sane, and the sanest people are really crazy?"

"Have you noticed that?"

"Where does that leave us?"

"I'm so lonely," she blurted out.

I wanted to say I was sorry about Gwen. I wanted to console her. But I had my own loss. The most I could manage was: "You two were really close."

"I never had a friend before." She was quiet for a minute. "Did you know she pulled out her hair?"

"What?"

Louise nodded, "They discovered it when they did the surgery on her hip. Trichotillomania, it's called."

"Who discovered what?"

"The nurses discovered it when they undid her braid. Her scalp was all torn up. Little raw patches."

"Trick-o-rex?"

"Trichorrhexomania. Hair-pulling disorder. Not to be confused with trichophagia—hair-eating disorder. They're both obsessive-compulsive behaviors. Mostly women get them."

"Surprise."

"It's why she wore the braid all the time. To cover the bald patches."

"Bald?"

"Little bald patches."

"Oh." I looked intently at Louise. She glanced out the window. I said, "You knew about this?"

She said, "The counselors told us in group. They wanted everyone to know so it wouldn't go undetected again."

I said, "But you knew before."

"Yes. Gwen told me on my first day. She hadn't meant to. It just slipped out. It's what made us friends. We knew the worst about each other."

Louise and I sat in silence for a long time. I kept remembering Gwen's slippery, diaphanous hair. I remembered Maeve in Brigham's, trying to put it up with the headband I'd stolen. I wondered what Maeve would think about a hair-pulling disorder. She would have something smart, something fresh to say. I looked over at Louise. I could see the weight of her grief dragging on her, like extra pounds.

I said, "I hated you." Quiet. Not even mean.

"I know."

"You didn't like me either."

"No. Not until the mall. That was nice, the presents."

"I was just trying to hide my feelings for Maeve." I watched Louise's face. I didn't want to seem more noble than I'd been. I said, "It was camouflage. I hadn't meant to get you or Gwen anything."

"I know. We all knew, Alice. Still, it was nice. You could have done it another way. You could have given Maeve the gift in private. But you didn't."

"Everyone knew?"

"Yes."

"Maeve knew?"

"Maeve always knows who likes her."

"How come you know so much about everyone all of a sudden?"

Louise shrugged. "Fat people have a lot of time for reflection."

"This is more than just reflection."

She shrugged again. "Some people surround themselves with thin friends. Or pretty friends. It makes them feel better about themselves. Some people, it makes them feel worse." She stared at her hands in her lap. "It wasn't like I had a lot of people competing for my friendship. Now they're both gone." She looked up at me. "You're the only one left that I like."

I said, "Do you know anything about Maeve's family?"

"Not much."

"She said something to me once about her father screwing around and that he broke one of her brothers' arms. Is that true?"

"She told me she was an only child. That she never knew her dad."

It was humiliating being lied to. "Why do you suppose she lies so much?"

"I think maybe she doesn't know what else to do."

"I miss her," I said.

"I know," said Louise. "I miss Gwen."

Forty

———

Two nurses brought a machine to weigh me in bed. A giant industrial hammock attached to a metal crane. They wheeled it over, rolled me on my side, laid the canvas flat, then rolled me back. They cranked and it lifted me off the bed, barely an inch, but enough. I was wondering why they hadn't made me step on a regular scale—I could still get out of bed and they loved to make me—when Nurse arrived. I asked her. She said the psychiatrist didn't want me knowing what I weighed.

Late in the afternoon I started thinking about Maeve, about whether I would ever see her again, and I hyperventilated. My whole chest constricted, and I thought, Here it is, the heart attack, only the monitor didn't sound any alarm, even after I banged it, so instead of just letting it come, without resisting, as I had told myself I would, I pressed the nurses' call button. I was terrified. A male nurse came right away and right away saw my distress and wrapped two pale hairy arms around me. Tufts of black fur stood out between each knuckle on the hands that he cupped around my mouth. I wondered if it were common for people trying to end their lives to scare themselves to death.

The nurse was very nice about it afterward, pretending the same thing had happened to him once, pretending that my fear had not revealed a lack of faith, a weakness of will. He stayed and chatted for several minutes (the nurses in the step-down unit never sat), and he was so pleasant and reassuring, I would never have guessed that he had tattled, if

my cardiologist, Dr. Anderson, hadn't shown up unexpectedly that same afternoon. He'd already made his morning
visit.

"I would be remiss if I didn't admit I was greatly
concerned." Dr. Anderson was my father's age, though
smaller and more reserved, with a pointy Adam's apple in a
long, wrinkleless throat. He coughed and his Adam's apple
danced wildly.

"There are complications with TPN. We are anxious
to get you off it as soon as possible."

"What kind of complications?"

"Your body is unable to process all the glucose.
There is way too much sugar in your blood. Today we found
it in your urine."

The Adam's apple was a visual accompaniment to
Dr. Anderson's speech; it went up at the beginning of sentences, down in the middle, and up again, even higher, at the
end.

"We're going to start you on insulin, to help your
pancreas along. Every six hours we'll test your blood and,
depending on your sugar levels, we'll give you a shot of
insulin."

"After all those years of not eating sweets."

"We can't keep you on TPN indefinitely. You've got
to start . . . well . . . eating." He coughed and his throat
leapt again. "Can I ask you something—it's not my place—
but I can't help wondering—I'm not a psychiatrist—I
can't tell you how many anorexics I've treated—but still, in
all these years—what I want to know is—why won't you
eat?"

"I can't."

"That's not an answer."

"Yes it is, really. I've lost my appetite."

"What would it take to get it back?"

"I don't know, it's not like losing your voice and
you just drink tea with honey and wait for it to come back.

It's more like . . . a kind of physical amnesia. That's it. I can't even remember being hungry. It's like I never was."

"Pardon me," he said. "But I think that's an awful lot of crap."

Forty-one

———

Syd came. They wouldn't keep her from me now. She brought knitting. I'd never seen her knit before. She sat in the chair beside my bed and held the needles tightly. She counted the number of stitches in the last row, her lips moving. There were pouches under her eyes.

"I heard they're having a memorial for that girl who died."

"Gwen?"

"Of course the family already had a service. But they're doing something here. For you girls. And the staff. Apparently, the staff is taking it very hard."

"I bet."

"I mean it."

"So do I."

"What was she like?"

"Unobtrusive. Sincere."

"I overheard someone say she was quite pretty."

"Not pretty. She had an old-fashioned look. What's the word?"

"Do you want to go to the memorial?"

"Not really."

"Why not?"

"Sublime, that's it. Rather than pretty."

"I would go with you. It's in the chapel downstairs. If you wanted."

"Syd, can I ask a question?"

"Certainly."

"You don't seem too upset by all this. I mean. Of course you're upset. You've been crying. But I was expecting a little . . . drama. A veil or something."

"Your father told me this wasn't happening *to me*, it was happening *to you*, and I should act accordingly."

"How very psychological of Dad. I guess this means you've spoken to him?"

"I didn't want to call him, but I had no choice. He's on one of his weekends. Only it's a week. In Spain. They're retracing Hemingway's steps. But he's leaving early."

"I wish you hadn't."

"And your psychiatrist agrees with your father's assessment."

"Absolute cretin."

"Why do you say that?"

"He makes the nurses weigh me every day and then not tell me what I weigh. As if the number would give me too much satisfaction."

"By all means, let's get the number." Syd stood and put her knitting on the chair. "How ridiculous for you not to have the number." She strode out of the room, her shoulders braced, unable to keep herself from this small flourish. I closed my eyes. I was tired.

She returned with an orderly who lugged a heavy upright hospital scale. She directed him to put it next to my bed.

"Syd—"

"I asked the nurses. They said you were perfectly capable of getting up."

"You've made your point."

"Get up."

"You're embarrassing me."

"In front of whom? It's just us here. I'm trying to save you from the frightful possibility of being denied the knowledge of how much you've shrunk to."

"Syd—"

"It's like winning the race without getting the prize."

"Enough."

"*I said get up!*"

I pushed the covers back. Why did people always feel like they had to teach you lessons? I was wearing two johnnies, back to front, front to back, so my behind was covered. My knees looked like fists. The nails on my toes were overgrown. I stepped on the scale, felt the shock of its metal stand. My legs were covered with a fresh layer of black hair. Syd played with the blocks. Three pounds less than ninety. Less than I thought.

"Well, now, that *is* an accomplishment for a girl who's five eleven."

"Five ten and three-quarters."

"I hope you're pleased."

"Quit it already."

"Will you be kind enough to tell your mother what you're trying to accomplish?"

"I'm not trying to accomplish anything."

"What I don't understand, Alice, is that for some girls it's all they can do—get skinny. You've always had so much going for you—looks, intelligence, personality."

"I have never had looks, and don't you dare suggest I have. The last thing I want at my memorial is people commenting on what a pretty girl I was. And you know as well as I do that personality is a consolation prize, the fruit of an unpretty life. All I've ever been is smart, and apparently, not smart enough. Or I wouldn't be in this position."

"Your narcissism—really. I don't know if I can bear it anymore."

"My narcissism? My narcissism!" I was shouting. "How dare you, of all people, accuse me of narcissism."

Two nurses and an orderly had gathered at the door.

"Look, Alice, just because you hate the way you look doesn't mean you're not a narcissist. You're still in the mirror all day. You're still looking."

Forty-two

———

Gert and Dana officially invited me to Gwen's memorial. They asked me to speak. I could see what they were thinking: Get her to commit to an event in her future.

"And what would I speak about?"

"Anything you like," said Dana. "Your fondest memory of Gwen."

"I don't have a fondest memory."

"That's a little unkind," said Gert.

"You're forgetting, I'm not especially kind."

"No, you're not." Gert glared at me from where she stood at the foot of the bed.

I could see her satisfaction. She'd been holding back. Dana put a hand on Gert's arm.

I said, "Who else will be there?"

"We've invited everybody." There was a certain note in Dana's voice. A hook she was dangling.

"Who is everybody?"

"All the girls who were on Gwen's unit. Even the ones who have since left."

I could feel the color burning up my face.

Forty-three

I asked Nurse if she smelled something fetid and got a second sponge bath for the asking. She was on her lunch break, visiting from cardiac care, and I was touched that she'd offered to work on her own time. She said I had no smell whatsoever. She used a gravelly oatmeal soap that scratched my skin, and I could feel the layer of dead cells peeling off. I felt lighter after. She patted everything dry and used a familiar, masculine-smelling talcum powder that successfully covered the rankness. It made me think of the time Dad brought me and Alex to the barbershop for haircuts. Afterward, the barber used a wood-handled brush with soft white bristles to brush our necks with talc. We three arrived home with identical haircuts and Syd got mad.

When Nurse left, two regular shift nurses came to inspect and clean my catheter. Dr. Anderson had implanted a central line catheter in my chest the day before—local anesthesia, one, two, three, but a sensitive enough procedure to require the operating room. Dr. Anderson wanted to run the TPN through the central line. He said they preferred this setup for long-term, high-volume intravenous anything. It gave them instant access with less mess. The phlebotomists were delighted. No more hours spent slapping at the veins in my wrists, hoping to make them rise. No more shameful, gorgeous bruises in purple, yellow, and green. But it felt strange. I thought, For the rest of my life I will have this opening in my chest, this functional wound. I wanted to tell Maeve. I wanted just to hear her voice.

When the nurses were finished, I told them I'd like to go for a walk. They exchanged approving looks and helped me with my Seaview slippers. At last I had my very own pair. One of them repositioned the heart monitor so it would not get in my way as I walked and then escorted me down the hall, her hand above mine on the IV pole. She was the motherly type, all bosom and anecdotes. When we got within sight of the elevators, I said, "I think I can manage."

She looked doubtful that I could pull the metal pole myself, but she left me to it. She went back to the nurses' station, which was several feet behind us, and sat there watching. I headed toward the pay phones, which were just to the right of the elevators.

The pole was harder to move than I thought. Mary Beth had said that if we concentrated all our mental energy on the muscles necessary for a particular exercise, we would go faster and farther. I closed my eyes and drew every ounce of strength into my right arm. The pole dragged along. One of the phones was taken by a doctor just out of surgery, those silly blue paper boots still covering his shoes. I used the phone nearest the elevators. It was set low to be in easy reach of people in wheelchairs, and I had to stoop to dial. I asked information for Maeve Sullivan. During all our time together, I'd never found out where she lived.

"What city, please?"

"I don't know. Could you try them all?"

"No, ma'am."

"How about Boston proper, then."

There were no listings for a Maeve Sullivan, but there were thirteen M. Sullivans. I tried to remember Sean's last name. He'd been Sean D. at Seaview. Then I remembered his brother Pat's amiable introduction.

"Could you try Sean Donovan?"

"In what city?"

Sean had to live near the Depot if he went there every night. "Marshfield, please."

I called a second time to get the operator to repeat

the number so I could memorize it. Syd's calling card I knew by heart. After three rings, someone picked up the phone. A woman.

"Maeve?" I said.

"Who's this?"

I dropped the phone. The nurse who had been watching stood up and leaned over the counter. I could hear Maeve's tinny voice bleating from the dangling receiver. My heart pounded against my chest. In their clinical discussions, the doctors referred to it as an anorexic heart. I wondered how they pictured it: small, miserly, beating itself to death against my concave chest, a pigeon's heart? A frog's, the kind we took from numbed bodies in seventh grade? Blood-less, frail. But it wasn't. I reached for the phone and put it back on the cradle. I couldn't catch my breath.

This time, the heart monitor rang and they all came running. Six of them or more. Thick, white soles thudded against the floor. People were just stepping off the elevator. They hung back, frightened by the sounds, the shouting nurses. I was on a table. I was flying down the hall. I was in the air, being passed hand over hand, from table to bed.

They pulled the johnny straight up, covering my face and neck, exposing my chest. Cold fingers and a colder metal stethoscope felt for my heart. I smelled someone's hair.

"I have it, I have it," a woman yelled.

The johnny separated my head from my body. A piece of the cotton cloth was stuck in my opened mouth.

"False alarm!"

The cardiac care people always shouted, like team-mates making sure every player had heard the score. "Tachycardia, not arrest," yelled the woman. "Panic, not ar-rest." The monitor was very sensitive. It had reacted to my excessive heart rate. "What's she weigh? The exact num-ber?"

They argued about the proper amount of sedative. I heard Dr. Anderson give the final order, his voice modulated and flat. When they'd injected the sedative, he pulled the johnny down and covered my chest. Dr. Anderson sat on the edge of the bed and held my hand, waiting for it to take effect. He talked about his son who was applying to colleges but wouldn't sit still long enough to do the applications. My eyes felt huge in my head, and although I couldn't quite follow what he said, I watched his Adam's apple bob.

Forty-four

———

Louise brought our body drawings to hang on my wall. Hers, mine, Gwen's, and Maeve's. She said she'd asked permission the day I left and it had taken them this long to decide. The scrolls were cumbersome, and she did a funny dance trying to tape them up. Finally she went for help and came back with a nurse's aide, a young thing who was not yet schooled in hiding her disdain. She held a corner of Louise's drawing against the wall and fed Louise pieces of tape. Louise sweat heavily as she bent to tape each corner, then along the sides. The young aide looked from Louise to the drawing to Louise again. Her nostrils flared with incredulity. I wanted to hit her on the mouth. To bloody her punctilious nose. It was a painful half hour, watching her watch Louise huff and puff around the drawings. At last the aide left. The entire wall facing my bed was covered.

"So you won't get lonesome," Louise said.

"What about you?"

"I'll come visit." She touched the back of her plump hand to her forehead. "Alice, I'm leaving soon."

"You too?"

"Afraid so."

"When?"

"A week from today."

She sat in the armchair next to my bed. She almost fit. Side by side, we watched the drawings, like spectators at an athletic event.

Louise had scratched the universe out of the black

crayon outline of her body. Careful constellations. I recognized Orion, Cassiopeia, the Milky Way, and two Dippers.
There were bits of other colors in the blackness, mostly green
and gold.

I said, "The internal landscape is a bit bleak, dear.
The universe rather one-dimensional. Do you follow me
when I say 'internal landscape'?"

We laughed harder than we should have. We
laughed so hard Louise was forced to help me to the bathroom, both of us crumpled over. Just inside the door, the
dam burst and a stream of colorless pee ran down my legs.
Louise jumped back so as not to soil her shoes. Which set off
another round of laughter. We clutched at our stomachs. I
peed even harder. Louise got a nurse to clean me up. When I
came out of the bathroom, Louise was in the chair again, her
eyes red, the hilarity gone. She was looking at the drawings.
She said, "I wish you'd eat."

Gwen's drawing was mostly as I remembered it, all
head and feet. Huge hair with canary-colored feathers. Those
patent-leather duct-tape shoes. There were two things I
hadn't seen before. She'd lipsticked on a brick red mouth. It
wasn't crayon or paint. One corner was smudged. I recognized the color as the same one that Janine had worn at my
first mixed meeting. Perhaps it was an institutional tube of
lipstick, handed down from one departing Seaview patient
to another. It made her mouth look firmer, more resolute
than it had been. And at the bottom of the paper in block
letters, she'd written out her name, GWENDOLYN.

My own drawing was the least accomplished. I'd
tried to replicate my cardiovascular system. But there was no
coherence. Just obscure lines running in all directions inside
the thinning outline. I was surprised by my own dullness.
Especially next to Maeve. Her drawing was predictably the
loudest, though also incomplete. Medusa's tangled hair in
thick purples and gold. Red shoulders leading to blue arms,
bright pink hands. The papier-mâché work was not meticu-
lous; the parts she'd finished—hair, arms, legs, and one pro-

digious breast—stood out in a lumpy, three-dimensional display. It gave me that hollow feeling. My joints ached. I wanted to put something inside.

I asked Louise to take a walk. We got two doors past my room. I told her I needed some time alone. She offered to escort me back, but I said I was fine. She took a step, then stopped. She wrapped two massive arms around me. It felt like I could count my bones in her embrace. When she pulled back, I kissed her on the cheek. She said, "I'll see you at Gwen's memorial." It was part directive, part plea. I didn't try to move until she'd gotten on the elevator.

The pole had gotten heavier since my last excursion. The nurses were never in sight when you needed something off-the-record, personal. All the weight was at the bottom of the pole, a pump inside a metal box, and I had to push it with my feet. Push-step-push-step-push-step. Odd that they didn't worry about the calories I burned during walks. By the time I got inside my room, sweat had collected on my eyelids and upper lip.

Louise had hung Maeve's drawing closest to the door. Maeve stood as she did in real life, feet planted, head up. I wanted to close the door, even touched my slippered foot to the rubber doorstop, but I couldn't budge it. I took small steps until I was facing her, my eyes at her chin. She hadn't done her features yet. I pictured the mouth curling into a sneer. I let go of the IV pole and leaned forward, my whole body reaching, as hers had once reached for mine, and fell into the papier-mâché. I rested there, tasting flour and water and glue. No Pluie this time. And none of the sooty smell hidden underneath. No water-plumped skin. No soft rolls to cushion the blow with my bone-hard self. For certain, it wasn't Maeve, but I stayed there anyway, comforted.

When the nurses found me, they lifted me straight into bed and shot a special something into my IV and I slept.

Forty-five

———

When I awoke, a young man was sitting in the chair next to my bed. I watched him through half-opened eyes. He was reading. It was Ronald Tillman and he was different from how I remembered him. Thicker. He had a man's body. A man's neck. He got up and went over to the drawings hanging on the wall. I considered the possibility that he was a dream.

"You look different," I said.

He turned around. "So do you." His hair was cut so short it was almost a shave. The cut gave him a high, square forehead.

"You're older," I said.

"Eight years."

"I haven't seen you in eight years?"

"It's ridiculous, I know."

"What are you doing here?"

"Syd called me."

"I'm sorry."

"I'm not."

"She must be desperate."

"I would say that's an accurate assessment."

He wasn't a dream. I managed a little smile. It was so good to see him. I said, "So tell me about your life."

He sprang back to the bed. He was graceful and sturdy. I could see the muscles in his neck. Prettier than me. He'd always been. He put the book on the floor—*Continental Drift*, it said on the cover—and pulled the chair nearer until it touched the bed. I dropped my hand and he took it. His hands were strong and elastic. All at once his eyes filled, and he leaned over to whisper in my ear, "You look terrible."

I nodded. There was so much surprise in his voice. I said, "We'll talk about it later. Tell me now about the last eight years. What do you do? How's your family?"

He collected himself. "They're good. They're comfortable for the first time. Now that they're not paying my tuition bills. They're completely pissed with me because after I got my Ph.D., I decided I wanted to write a novel instead of teach English. My mother calls once a week to rage about my being downwardly mobile."

"So what's the novel about, or am I not supposed to ask?"

"You're not supposed to ask."

"Not even an old girlfriend, like me?"

His eyes filled again, and he laid his cheek against the palm of my hand, which was flat on the edge of my bed. His face darkened in relief against the hospital sheets.

I whispered, "Come on. Doesn't Felicitas mean happy or joy or something?"

He spoke without lifting his head. He said, "We took awfully good care of each other then."

"I never would have made it through high school."

"How did we even manage to find each other?"

"Divine intervention, it must have been. God's only kindness during puberty."

"Did you hear that Sister Geraldine died?"

"No."

He sat up. "A year ago. Breast cancer." He looked around for a tissue. There was a box on my minibureau.

"How old was she?"

"Forty-something."

"You mean she was in her thirties when she taught us? She seemed so ancient."

"I know." He blew his nose.

"What a waste."

"Which? Her dying so young?"

"Yes," I said. "What else?"

"I don't know. Everything."

"What everything?"

"It seems particularly cruel for her to have had breast cancer. After all she'd given up."

"You know what they say. Sacrifice is its own reward."

We sat in uncomfortable silence. He massaged his eyelids. His fingers were long and the webs between them ash-colored. After a pause, he said, "So tell me, what have you been doing? Before this."

"I'm an archivist at Boston College. I started right after graduation."

"Sounds great."

"It isn't. I mostly sort papers."

"You got your masters?"

"Still getting it."

He nodded.

I said, "I have a feeling you know all this."

He hesitated. "Syd told me. We had coffee."

"Really? Where?"

"At her house."

"I hope she let you keep your shoes on."

"She did."

"How very liberal of Syd."

"Come on, Alice, she's not that bad. She's always treated me well."

"Because you were such a novelty."

"To you too, at first."

"At first."

Ronald got up from the chair and walked over to the body drawings. We both felt awkward and angry. He studied the portraits. He touched the crayon, feathers, papier-mâché. He stood very close, then as far back as possible. For a second, I wished I'd done things differently. I wished I'd told him more in high school. After that time we'd had sex. I wished I hadn't waited to get to Seaview to talk about certain feelings, or to listen to talk about them, because even at Seaview I avoided discussing things.

Suddenly I had an almost overwhelming urge to tell him now. To talk at length about the emptiness—our leitmotif at Seaview. If anyone could understand, it would be Ronald. Not understand in the way the counselors did, which was to take every word and action apart and lay them bare, to focus attention on every inch of your life until it was brittle with apparent meaning. With cause and effect. Ronald, I knew, could respect the mystery of what I'd felt and what I'd done. So I almost told him right then and there about the emptiness that the overeaters tried to fill with impossible amounts of food, again and again; the emptiness that the bulimics tried to disgorge, as if it had been caught, a chicken bone or a fragile green fish's gill in their quivering throats; the emptiness which we anorexics, in our superior knowledge and practice, tried to constrict, tried to compress by strangulation and deprivation, tried to irradiate with nothing, with time, with consistent daily loss, that trapdoor of emptiness which I tried instinctively to make collapse into itself years before I knew of Louise's black holes, years before I could picture in my mind's eye that enormous whoosh of nothing sucking nothing into smithereens, into a number of infinitesimally small value, into zero volume, zero density. Gone.

But I didn't. I let the moment, like others, pass. I asked Ronald to get me a fresh cup of water. He went off down the hall and when he returned with a new plastic cup and a long, accordion-pleated straw, I took a sip, my lips forming a tiny beak around the tip. I was jolted by the cold metal taste of the water. My lips were dry. I said, "So what's the novel about?"

"I told you, you're not supposed to ask."

"Look. At the rate I'm going, I'll never read it."

"It's a coming-of-age story."

I could hear the resentment in his voice. I said, "Autobiographical?"

"Yes and no."

"Am I in it?"

"Why is that the first question people ask?"

"It was my second question, and I guess I want to know if I was as important to you as you were to me."

"In fact you're the most likable character in the book. You help the protagonist figure out his true identity."

"I do?"

"You're carefully disguised, of course. You have blond hair instead of black."

"I'm sure no one will recognize me."

He laughed lightly.

I said, "And what's the protagonist's true identity?"

"Oh, you know." He looked at me.

"Obviously I don't."

He sighed, then smiled. "Black fag growing up in white suburbia."

It was something I'd known my whole life, but had never, not even once, told myself. I felt the enormity of my own self-deception. It made me sad. And a little embarrassed. What I'd missed. What I'd kept myself from knowing. I said, "When?"

"Always."

I tried to think what things I'd always known about myself. I said, "If you knew, why did we —"

"It was a kind of confirmation. I figured since I loved you so much, if there were any chance of it working with girls, it would have worked with you."

I knew, intellectually, that it shouldn't have stung, but it did. I said, "Well, that makes me feel, well, superfluous."

His face looked smaller, younger. "It shouldn't. I mean. I don't want it to. You were never, not for a day in my life, superfluous."

"If something happens more than once, is that a trend? I've slept with two people and afterward, they both left."

He took a piece of paper out of his front pocket and carefully unfolded it. There were many creases. "Here. I saved this."

I recognized the paper. Syd's expensive cream stationery. We were forbidden to use it. I had torn off the edges to give it a handmade look. It was still thick to the touch.

Felicitas,

I have given your proposal much thought. What is innocence if not unknowing? If not ignorance? A sacred trust worth spilling. If we are Perpetually afraid of losing our unknowingness, we remain forever afraid of Life. I would rather share the shedding of our innocent ignorance together than find myself depending, as T.W. said, on the kindness of strangers. This biblical Knowing of each other can only bring greater knowing of our separate selves.

Perpetua

Reading the letter made me cry. I had such dim recognition of that girl, that voice. I looked at Ronald. He was crying too, his face younger and smaller still. I remembered at the movies that night, after we had had sex, he had cried at Jill Clayburgh's desertion by her husband. While I ate the popcorn, he had used all our napkins as tissues.

Before leaving, he kissed me on the cheek, and said, "Whoever she is, she's not worth a hair on your head."

Forty-six

I dreamt they were forcing something down my throat. Something thick and plastic, too big for my narrow passageway. A giant accordion straw. Two people held down my shoulders and a third knelt on my bed, shoving the plastic thing down with both hands. "Swallow, swallow," the one on top said. "Atta girl, come on now, swallow, swallow." I woke up clutching my throat.

A man was there, a doctor or one of the male nurses, I couldn't tell. He stood in the shadow of the door, his silhouette framed by the light in the hall. He said, "It was just a dream, there, there. Just a dream."

I said, "They were putting a huge plastic pipe down my throat."

He said, "It's a respirator, that's all. You're remembering the respirator. It's not a dream, but a memory. After the heart attack, they surely put you on a respirator."

"That's right," I said. Syd had told me they did.

"Exactly," he said, rubbing his fat hands together. With the fingers laced, they looked like a small, edible bird. I knew it was Dr. Paul hiding his shame in the darkness.

My mouth was dry as smoke, but I sucked in the juices from every corner of my body and spat. Now I'll die from dehydration, I thought. But he left.

Forty-seven

I had three different fantasies about Maeve's return. Scenarios, really, that I painstakingly developed, day after day, adding details until I could play them back in my mind like movies. In each scenario she returned, significantly, on the day, or eve, of Gwen's memorial.

In the first, she wore a nurse's uniform, stolen, or bought at the Salvation Army. It was out of style, as uniforms go, too short, with a wide zipper down the length of the front. A size-too-small seventies dress with huge collar flaps so big they were practically lapels. Her breasts showed where the zipper didn't zip all the way; her flesh pushed at the seams. She had gained weight. She had stopped throwing up altogether.

It was night, and she had snuck into the hospital and onto my floor, no silly nurse's cap but the obligatory white hose and shoes. When her thighs came together I could hear the scratch of the nylon meeting. She had come to take me away. The first thing she said was, "You look like shit."

We fought for a minute the way couples do when they know they will be making up. I said, "What took you so long?"

She said, "I had to pull the outfit together."

"And this was the best you could do?"

"Shut up and get dressed."

She brought me clothes. Soft cotton pants and a light sweatshirt top that were easy on my skin. She swore when she saw the yellow and green bruises up and down my arms, cursing the doctors on my behalf. On the wall of machinery behind my bed, Maeve found the setting for my heart monitor and turned it to OFF. I rested the monitor on the end of the bed. I insisted on wearing the Seaview slippers.

She had commandeered a wheelchair. As she bent to snap the footrests in place, I looked down the well of her cleavage and felt the shock of desire between my legs. I reached down and touched a breast with my withered bone-finger. I wanted to unzip the dress; I wanted her breasts to fall out of their polyester encasement with a heavy plop, like melons off the back of a truck. I wanted her to lift them to my shrunken face. Instead she stood and touched her hand to my cheek, her fingers tracing the sharp line of my jaw as she pulled away.

She tucked two blankets around me. She put a baseball cap on my head, its bill falling immediately over my eyes. Carefully she disengaged the IV from my catheter, letting the sugar-water spill onto my bed, soaking the sheets and the lamb's wool square. She wheeled me past the nurses' station and onto the elevator. In the parking lot, I spied Pat's rattling truck. She helped me out of the chair and up the big step into the familiar cab. I didn't ask her how she'd gotten it. I didn't ask her where we were going. I picked at the yellowed stuffing growing out of the holes in the upholstery. Once inside, she took off the ugly shoes and white hose and drove barefoot, her toes pointing, her insteps arching with each clutch and acceleration. As she drove, I watched the short nurse's dress climb up her thigh.

In the second scenario, she came an hour before Gwen's memorial service, in the bright of day. She wore the same pair of leather pants she had worn the first time I saw her, the same plunging angora sweater, only everything tighter. She'd gained weight. The first thing she said was, "You look like shit."

We fought like a couple intent on inflicting pain.

I said, "You've gotten fat."
She said, "I've stopped throwing up altogether."
"So fat is better?"
She said, "Sean has a very big dick."
"Gulliver, I'm sure. He uses it to put out fires."
"To start them."
"Why are you doing this?"
"I don't want you to starve to death over me."
"You flatter yourself."
"I'm not worth it."
"Talk about understatement."
"You look like you're ready to die."
"And will you two live happily ever after?"
"I think you should come to Gwen's memorial."
"I think you should leave."

When she did leave, her ass like a watermelon in her too tight pants, I got up and removed the IV from the catheter, letting the glucose syrup spill on the floor. I went over to the wall of machinery behind my bed and found the setting for the heart monitor. I turned it off, then left the innocuous-looking monitor on the pillow on my bed. I walked unencumbered and barefoot to the body drawings on the wall. I pulled hers off in long strips. When the nurses found me, I was unconscious on the floor, surrounded by papier-mâché.

In the third scenario, Maeve came two hours before Gwen's memorial service, in the bright of day. She wore a nurse's dress similar to the one in the first scenario only it was Sean's little sister's dress from when she had worked at a bakery. Maeve was working at a bakery. She'd gained weight. The first thing she said was, "You look like shit."

We fought like couples who do not know why they are fighting.

I said, "Your legs look like the trunks of trees in those hose."

Maeve had stopped throwing up, but she said it was

only temporary. Sean's dick was medium to small. She had fucked Sean's brother Pat once in the cab of the pickup truck, the stuffing from the upholstery getting stuck in her hair, the hard edges of the torn vinyl cutting into her skin. Pat's dick was definitely bigger. She would stay with Sean until just before she started puking again, then she would move in with Pat. The brothers would never be friends again. She would manage a month or more with Pat before it would start up again. She would leave the first time the toilet backed up.

I said, "What about me?"

She said, "I think the difference between fucking men and fucking women is that I want to *have* the men I fuck and I want to *be* the women. See? That's why I could never fuck women full-time. I mean, I need that sense of self I get back from Sean. I see myself, I see him. Myself. Him. It's easy. But with women, there's this, what do you call it, slippage, I don't know. The first time it happened I was sixteen. The woman was a cook in this restaurant where I waitressed. I felt like I'd crossed over to the other side. It was fucking thrilling, like getting really, really stoned, like seeing the earth from the moon. But then I panicked: What if I can't get back? What if I get marooned here? It's too much work for me."

I said, "I'm not *women*. I'm Alice."

She said, "Nonetheless."

I said, "I want you to lie on top of me."

She said, "You'll love other women."

I said, "I don't want to."

"But you will."

I said, "Please lie on top of me."

She said, "I'll crush you. You'll suffocate."

"Yes."

She removed the rubber doorstop and closed the door. She shut off the overhead fluorescent light, drew the curtain, and took off her shoes. There were holes in the hose by each of her big toes. She climbed into bed on the side without the IV pole. I had to move the heart monitor so it lay on top of my chest, instead of at my side. The bed tipped. She threw a white-stockinged leg over both of mine, scrunched her long body until it curled into me, her head at the base of my neck, the tip of her nose grazing a collarbone. I felt moist air slipping in and out of her nostrils. I sunk under the weight of her flesh, under the heat of her breasts. I breathed as though I were meditating, short shallow drafts that unexpectedly sufficed. Her voluptuous hair spilled over my body. I could see she dyed it. I moved several strands away from the catheter and put the ends in my mouth. I lifted the hair at the nape of her neck and sniffed the dampness there. We lay like this for exactly one hour. I counted each minute on the clock on the wall. Maeve's breathing got regular and it's possible she slept. I stayed entirely conscious. When the hour was up, she left.

But Maeve did not come. I waited, still not eating. Days went by. Another week. I whittled myself down to absolute essence, waiting for her. I fought with Syd. My father called from the airport in Madrid where he'd been delayed. I made him cry. Ronald sent flowers, the only one to bother. Everyone tried to get me to eat or, at least, to go to Gwen's memorial, where, I assumed, they figured I'd encounter the Cold Reality of Death and repent. Instead, I counted on Maeve's return. It would be a climax. She would come on the day of Gwen's memorial and save me, or come and be the final push toward chaos. I had read that dying people often waited to finish some personal business before finally letting go. There were stages to death—shock, denial, anger, bargaining, and acceptance. Maeve was my bargain. I would accept whichever scenario came to pass as long as she returned. I was a little afraid of the chaos. But I was more afraid of her indifference.

By four-thirty on the day of Gwen's last hurrah, a half hour into the four o'clock service, my fear had turned into anger. I wasn't even worth a good-bye. I pictured her sitting next to Sean in the chapel downstairs, piously mourning Gwen. I slid my legs over the side of the bed. The blood in my veins seemed to slow. I felt a stiffness in my limbs. I felt my own stone-hardness.

It occurred to me that in some alternate universe all three of my scenarios were taking place simultaneously. All three plus this one, the real one, me climbing by myself out of bed, me turning off the heart monitor, then leaving it centered on the lamb's wool square, me yanking out the IV because the pole was too heavy to push, the useless meal dripping (not quite the spill I had envisioned) onto the floor beneath my bed. There was a universe where all possible permutations of life occurred at once, a universe where Maeve kidnapped me from Seaview, and left me for happiness with a man, and left me for unhappiness with various men, but mostly, with herself. But I did not live in that universe. Where desertion at least had meaning. I lived where Maeve had simply forgotten me.

I was furious, but I was bored and lonely too. Bored with not eating. Lonely from the emptiness, which I usually controlled by not eating, but which suddenly spread, kindled by my anger. For the first time in weeks, I didn't want—couldn't stand—to be alone. Of all these feelings, the only one that would do me any good was the anger. I whetted it.

I bent to pull the slippers on my feet and almost fainted from the change in altitude. My knees cracked, a loud popping sound like a cork. I retrieved Syd's gift-robe from the closet and wrapped the belt twice around before knotting it tightly, the hole in my chest neatly covered. At the threshold of my door, I waited for the coast to clear and tried not to feel dizzy.

My nearest neighbor was an elderly gentleman who'd survived a double bypass. I crept to his door, my skeletal back sliding against the wall, and saw what I needed just inside, a four-legged walker. It would support me to the elevator. He was sleeping. As I laced my spider fingers around the rubber hand grips of his walker, I heard a fortu-itous sound. Someone's heart monitor was ringing at the opposite end of the unit. During the ten-minute frenzy that ensued, I navigated my way toward the elevator.

On the first floor, I was a conspicuous arrival. When the elevator doors flung open, I paused, cowed by the explo-sion of noise that greeted me. A young man politely held the door, his hand across the rubber mechanism that sprang back and forth trying in vain to open. I didn't know why getting off took so much longer than getting on, but it did, and a sea of people gathered to one side as I disembarked. They wore lots of clothes, heavy sweaters and light jackets (it was the end of April but still not spring) and their cheeks were flushed with an outdoor chill. They stood silently as the walker, then I, descended. Their eyes traced a line from the metal legs to my wire arms and spine. I felt the weight of my skin.

I tried not to look left or right. I focused on the sign, suspended from the ceiling, at the end of the short hall, a square white electrified sign with red letters that spelled EXIT. Left at the sign and then I didn't know how many yards to the automatic glass door. Before I came to that, I would reach the Visitors' Information Desk and the gift shop. And straight across, the chapel. When I passed the exit sign, I could hear the hum of the automatic door. I felt the cold from outdoors insinuate itself up through the floor. The Seaview slippers were thin. I flexed the bones in each foot. I unfurled my toes. I wasn't sure what I would say to Maeve or to the others. The emptiness seemed to expand as I hur-ried, as best I could, around the corner. I smelled the parking lot.

Two arch-shaped wooden doors made up the chapel entrance. They were fifteen feet high with a single oversized antique doorknob that required two hands for opening. I stood with my walker and waited. I would have to catch someone coming out. The noise from inside was muffled, but I made out the parched drone of the visiting priest who had celebrated the one Mass I'd attended. It felt like years ago. I remembered the ruckus I'd caused just for asking; I remembered Gwen's fury as she passed my room on the way to breakfast, her white head flashing; I remembered Louise, always the diplomat, using her massive body to shield Gwen from my equally massive superiority and greed. I began to shiver.

A woman appeared. She wore a laminated nametag with a photo ID that said: *My name is EVELYN and I am a Seaview VOLUNTEER. How can I HELP you?* She'd been watching me from the Visitors' Information Desk. Without meeting my eyes, Evelyn gripped the giant doorknob with both hands and opened the door as far as it would go. She stood behind it, so the people inside saw the walker first. By the time I came fully into view, the congregants had turned where they stood in their pews and the priest, the old-timer, had stopped talking.

The small chapel was full, each of the six pews on either side stuffed with people. Although I usually avoided the exposure of a collective gaze, I didn't mind—I was beyond minding—their stares. I rested for a moment and stared back. It was comforting to see familiar faces. I immediately felt less lonely. On my left stood the folks from Seaview; on my right Gwen's family and friends. Unexpectedly, Syd was there, in the very first pew next to Louise, who was looking demolished. Gert and Dana stood in the pew right behind them.

I spied Hank up front on the right, with a couple who I assumed were Gwen's parents, the mother a bottled version of Gwen's white-blondness. Her shoulders were curved forward in the bird posture so particular to Gwen that I wondered whether she'd always had it, or whether she had inherited it, in some strange way, through Gwen's death, a reversal of the usual genetic transfer from generation to generation. She looked thin, too. The father had the baffled expression of someone recently incapable of speech, the puzzled, almost coherent brow of an early Alzheimer's

patient. The friends were the usual assortment. Oboe players, I guessed, well-intentioned trust-fund children and college roommates who'd honestly Had No Idea. There was a
woman with dark glasses and a cane, whose ear, not eyes,
was turned to the sound of my entrance. Most likely the
blind woman whom Gwen had read to each week before
she'd been spirited away to Seaview.

They all waited for me.

It was Gwen's service, I knew, Gwen's moment. But I
felt myself on the edge of stealing it. Syd was crying. I did
not have to see her to know.

I glanced back at the Seaview side. Amy was standing next to Queen Victoria, who looked grandmotherly and
healthy; she'd lost the orange sheen from the laxatives.
Penny and Penny's friends, the mustachioed weight lifter
and the triathlete, were all in the same pew with Mary Beth,
whose lips moved silently in some Zen prayer. No Maeve.
But she must be here. I began my walk forward. Crank and
rattle. It was as if some tiny nuts and bolts were loose in the
hollow metal frame of the walker. They jiggled with every
step, a single-toned accompaniment.

The old priest stepped off the altar and began walking my way. He was dressed as before, no robe, just the alb
and stole over black slacks, the ubiquitous collar. I hadn't
noticed the kindness in his face before, but it was visible
then, a softening of the deep rutted lines that had frozen his
features into a religious scowl. He stepped carefully around
the small table in the middle of the aisle on top of which
rested, not the gifts of the Mass, as was done at Most Precious Blood, not the Host-filled chalice, but a half a dozen
photographs of Gwen and a silver urn. I heard sobbing from
both sides. I thought to myself, She must not have been long
in the incinerator, her bones already part ash.

The old priest cupped his decrepit, spotted hand
around my elbow and urged me to abandon my walker. I felt
heat streaming from his fingertips. He left the walker directly behind the table supporting Gwen's literal and figura-

tive remains, making sure there was room to pass. Some of
the pictures of Gwen were from before the anorexia. One
with Hank. The priest squeezed my elbow, and I looked at
him. He was smiling.

All at once I realized that he had not been assigned
his hospital rounds, as I had imagined during my first visit;
he had chosen them. He hadn't been put out to pasture,
hadn't been banished to the least hopeful, most depressing
part of priestly life. The old-timer came to Seaview day after
day because he wanted to. I pictured the soft, thick oil of
extreme unction on his thumb. He was thorough and old
school, a lover of ritual; that thumb graced eyelids, then
nostrils, lips, palms, and the soles of curling feet. He had not
succumbed to the new and convenient and impersonal. He
would not make the sign of the cross on foreheads and be
done with it. He took responsibility for delivering life's last
intimacy. And it filled him.

This made me glad, that even one person could find
fullness.

At the front of the church, he left me off at Louise's
pew. Syd had moved back a row and Louise slid down,
making room. I sat, and the priest, back on the altar, nodded
to the congregation. They sat too. The priest raised his hands
above his head and for a full minute he just held them there.

There was no Communion. It was a memorial, not a
funeral Mass. And besides, not Catholic because Gwen
hadn't been. The priest was just doing his ecumenical best. I
had missed the first forty-five minutes, which had been filled
with testimonials about Gwen's positive influence in people's lives. The old priest spent the remaining half hour re-
hashing his Easter sermon, the one I had already heard.
Gwen's parents looked unconvinced that death was the antecedent to birth. He said the usual things about loss being a
part of an indecipherable divine plan. He looked at Gwen's
parents, and I could see he really felt for them. His dry eyes
roamed over our heads, searching. "It's who we become, in

time," he said, "an accumulation of our losses. It's all we have."

When it was over, he blessed Gwen's urn and then visited the parents. He shook their hands. He patted Hank on the back. Before leaving, he came over to me. He smiled, his face folding along the well-grooved lines. He took my hand in his. His thumbs felt huge.

I followed his slightly hunched back as he headed out of the chapel. This time, he had left his neat black trench coat folded in a square in the very last pew. When he bent to pick up his coat, a relative of Gwen's jumped up to open the doors. In the arched opening, framed by the bright fluorescents of the lobby, stood Maeve. She was wearing a short, white uniform, many years out of style. I could see the circles under her eyes. She looked tired. She took a pot of lip gloss from the deep front pocket of her uniform, which was one size too tight. The priest put his dark coat on over the alb and stole and passed through the chapel doors. Walking out, he momentarily blocked my view. In that instant, I lost sight of Maeve.

Immediately the mourners stepped into the chapel aisle, donning coats, shaking hands, discussing where they would go to eat. I was afraid that by the time I navigated through the crowd of people, Maeve would truly be gone, not just hidden behind the chapel door, but gone through the automatic glass door, into the parking lot, into whatever car or truck was waiting, its upholstery torn and depressing because it had been that way for many years. I was afraid that by the time I reached the chapel entrance, Maeve would have disappeared into a world where, when things broke, they stayed that way.

I tried just the same. Forsaking the walker, I crept along, spider fingers on the ends of the pews, touching shoulders, pulling sleeves, pushing more than once. Several Seaview people tried to talk to me. Little Amy approached, actually stood in my path and said hey, but I went around her. I concentrated, as Mary Beth had instructed, on the muscles necessary for such complex navigation. I put my head down, avoiding the eyes of the well-intended. I had seen Maeve! I was enraged and thrilled at once. I propelled my wasted body toward the chapel doors.

For the second time, my anorexia failed me. My progress was absurdly slow. Half the congregation—Gwen's family and friends—reached the door ahead of me, their nonchalance more powerful, more profluent than my most intense desire. I could only crawl toward the chapel doors. When I got there, Maeve was nowhere to be found. I was sure I would never see her again. After all this, after all the wanting and not wanting and trying-not-to-want, desire itself was a disappointment. It lacked agency. I had been afraid of it so long without realizing how ineffectual it could be. It was only a fact, like the color of Gwen's hair, the size of Louise's waist, the drooping shape of Maeve's breasts. Desire was a choice I could make or not. Nothing more. What I hadn't realized in these weeks since Gwen's death and Maeve's departure from Seaview was that I had already made it. Weeks and weeks ago. Not necessarily on the day that Maeve and I first met, but soon after. The first time I tried to impress her. The first moment I acknowledged, even if only to myself, that I wanted—no, needed—her absolute, undivided attention.

What seemed remarkable, finally, when I thought of it, was not that I loved women, but that I had loved a woman so imprecise. Maeve in all her chaos. This was what I would have said to her if she had been there at the chapel entrance when I reached it. That I loved her imperfection. But she wasn't there. What else could I do? I turned back to the few stragglers left inside.

Acknowledgments

A very good friend of mine tells me that the best art is not collaborative, not the product of consensus, but the product of a single vision. And though I do agree with him theoretically—the vision is mine, the choices are mine, and, ultimately, I must take responsibility for both—my experience of writing this book has been much more like collaboration than solitary inspiration. *The Passion of Alice* would not have been written without the patient literary guidance of Patricia Chao, Karin Cook, Allan Hoffman, and Kenneth King.

I offer special thanks to my teacher and mentor, Mona Simpson, who taught me to take myself seriously as a writer and whose staggering generosity I will never be able to repay.

I would like to thank Sloan Harris, Amanda Urban, and Dawn Seferian for believing in my book and doing the work of getting it published.

For help with research, I am indebted to Mary Conway-Spiegel, Katie Doran, Anne Kessler, M.D., Karen Langan, John Siegal, D.D.S., and Paul Rogers, R.N.

For time to write, I thank Cottages at Hedgebrook, the MacDowell Colony, and the Revson Fellows Program at Columbia University.

For help along the torturous road to a first novel, I thank Linsey Abrams, Denise Lewis, Joseph Olshan, Sarah Schulman, Pamela Rosenblum, and Jacqueline Woodson.

My love and thanks to all my friends who have cooked meals, bought dinner, and paid for movies, theater, and everything else that I have not been able to afford while writing this book.

I would like to thank the fabulous staffs, past and present, of the Lesbian and Gay Community Services Center, my spiritual home in New York City, especially Richard Burns, Donald Huppert, and Barbara Warren.

For their years of sustenance, both physical and spiritual, and for their seemingly boundless confidence in me, I thank my family: Jim and Edna Grant, Bill and Cindy Grant, and Jaime Grant and Tracy Conaty. And my grandmothers, Josephine Ahern Grant and Edna Reilly MacNeill, who would have loved to see this day.

And last but hardly least, I would like to thank my lover, Janet Leon, who gave me time to write, to make mistakes, and to keep on trying.

ABOUT THE AUTHOR

STEPHANIE GRANT received her M.A. at New York University and was a Revson Fellow at Columbia University. Currently she curates a reading series, "In Our Own Write," for emerging writers at the Lesbian and Gay Community Services Center. She lives in Brooklyn and is at work on a new novel.